THE Homecoming

THE DE MONTFORTES

DANELLE HARMON

Published by Oliver-Heber Books

0 9 8 7 6 5 4 3 2 1

Dedicated to my loving husband, Chris.

With special thanks to Lauren May for her insight, enthusiasm, and friendship, to Tanya Anne Crosby for—well, everything!—and to my Aunt Debbie, who gave little Turnip his name.

I am blessed.

The de Montfortes
CAST OF CHARACTERS AND THEIR BOOKS

Lucien de Montforte, His Grace the fifth duke of Blackheath

The Wicked One, *Book #4 in the de Montforte series*

Eva, his duchess

Their children:

Augustus, Marquess of Ravenscombe and heir apparent

Lord Charles de Montforte

The Beloved One, *Book #2 in the de Montforte series*

Amy, his wife

Their children:

Mary Elizabeth

Lord Gareth de Montforte

The Wild One, *Book #1 in the de Montforte series*

Juliet, his wife

Their children:

Charlotte

Gabriel

Lord Andrew de Montforte

The Defiant One, *Book #3 in the de Montforte series*

Celsiana ("Celsie"), his wife

Their children:

Laura

Justin

Lady Nerissa (de Montforte) O' Devir

Captain Ruaidri O' Devir, her husband

The Wayward One, *Book #5 in the de Montforte series*

Their children:

Aidan

Prologue

Newburyport, Massachusetts, 10 March, 1781

My dear brother, Lucien,

Greetings from our home here across the sea, where all is well, and I remain content and blessed. Little Aidan is thriving and Ruaidri has already introduced him to boats, something to which he took as readily as a de Montforte to a horse. Our new home reminds me in some ways of Gingermere, and the smell of salt air brings to mind memories of that place. Enough of my ramblings and I shall get straight to the point … I am dreadfully missing home and pining for my family. Ruaidri says he is willing to take me back for a visit now that you and Sir Roger have addressed and

settled the very issue that made it impossible for me to return to England. Of course, my dear husband worries for my safety, never his own, though surely, he's clever enough to get us safely across the sea despite the fact this tedious war is still dragging on. We will be leaving here in about a fortnight and hope to be at Blackheath Castle in time to see the roses blooming. Please let our brothers know we are coming so we can all gather together as one big family; I hope Charles and Andrew are looking forward to finally meeting Ruaidri as much as he is looking forward to finally meeting them. I miss and cannot wait to see you all.
— Nerissa

L ucien de Montforte, the fifth duke of Blackheath, pursed his lips on a little grin, folded the vellum, and holding it lightly between his fingers, moved to the library windows. He had read the letter—still smelling faintly of his sister's perfume—a dozen times, maybe a hundred. Run his fingers over her words, anticipated her homecoming, envisioned it in his mind, and carefully masked a boyish excitement he hadn't felt in some time.

Would today be the day?

Beyond his dark gaze, the downs fell away to the village of Ravenscombe a mile off in the distance, and a gentle spring breeze stirred the leaves of the old copper beeches that lined the moat. She would be coming through that gatehouse soon enough. *In time to see the roses blooming*, she had written. He looked at them now, planted around the gatehouse by his long-dead mother. Waiting, just as he was, tight red, white and pink buds thrusting up through shiny green leaves, ready to burst open any day now. Waiting. Like the whole family—already gathered here at the ancient family home—were waiting. Like the whole house with its five centuries of de Montforte history was waiting.

Waiting, for the prodigal daughter to come home.

A lifetime, it felt like, since she'd last walked these ancient rooms and halls. She, who had left here a maiden and was returning with a husband and child. And yet it had only been just over a year and a half.

He cast a glance at the road beyond the gatehouse. It was still empty, and by now the stage up from Southampton would have come and gone on its way to Oxford. Not today, then. Not today...

But soon.

Maybe tomorrow.

He sighed and looked out the ancient, mullioned windows at the lawn outside, his gaze seeking the two people he loved most in this world. Augustus, his son and heir, played on the lawn, his mother sitting in a chair nearby and watching him with a sharp eye. Beside her, the red setter Esmerelda lolled, tongue hanging out of her smiling mouth, a few grey hairs now sprinkling her eyebrows. Overhead, clouds drifted eastward, dropping shadows that rolled steadily in and out of the late afternoon sunlight in an ever-changing array of light and shadow.

Where was she right now?

Would it be today that her feet once again touched the shores of England?

Tomorrow?

Yes, he had "addressed" the matter that had kept his little sister exiled from her childhood home. Or rather, he thought wryly, *fixed* it. Her very faith in his supposed supernatural abilities to change the world were not exactly ... misplaced. Lucien had accomplished many impossibilities in his life—and would accomplish many more—but getting his little sister off the hook for bludgeoning a Royal Navy seaman in order to save her husband's life had taken every bit of his considerable influence and skill. It had been treason, pure and simple, and certain execution had awaited her if she'd ever set foot on England's shores again.

But the idea of Lady Nerissa de Montforte—that is, Nerissa O'Devir, he thought with a hard-earned acceptance—never seeing her ancestral home or her family again, was something that was beyond Lucien's ability to imagine or tolerate.

The idea of her child—in blood a de Montforte if in name he was something else— was equally intolerable.

He'd "fixed" it, all right.

And while Lucien might've gone to America a year and a half earlier with the sole intention of killing Ruaidri O'Devir and bringing his sister back home, he now knew with a certainty that if the unthinkable happened, and the clever Irish mariner who now captained a vessel for the American Continental Navy were to be caught by the Royal Navy, he would pull out every stop to save him just as he would any other member of the family.

But Ruaidri was wily and smart. He would never get caught.

The clouds thickened, and off in the distance, Lucien watched a dark band of rain moving steadily forward, ready to water those same roses that stood waiting, below. Best to go summon Eva and little Augustus before the clouds opened.

He cast one last wistful glance down the road beyond the gatehouse.

Empty.

He laid the letter on his desk, and turning, went to join his wife and son.

Chapter One

TWO DAYS LATER....

⁕

"Nerissa, *mo grá*. Ye look as nervous as a baby bird amidst a bunch o' starvin' cats. What ails ye, lass?"

The confines of the coach were cramped, and as Lady Nerissa O'Devir looked out at her homeland that she hadn't seen in over a year and a half, the majestic rolling downs spreading out as far as the eye could see, she smoothed her skirts and tried to muster a brave face.

"It is nothing, Ruaidri," she assured him, flashing a smile that didn't fool him one bit. "But I worry that I have put you ... put all of us, in danger by coming here. You were the Irish Pirate, wreaking hell against British shipping back in Boston ... you're an officer in the American Navy ... and I—"

"Have faith that if yer brother told us he's 'fixed' things, then he has."

She nodded, holding little Aidan close to her bosom as the coach bumped over the muddy chalk road. Across from her, Ruaidri, handsome in his unassuming bottle-green coat and fawn breeches, his thick, wildly curling black hair caught in a queue and his tricorn on the seat beside him, held a warm body in his own lap, but it was no child. Or at least, no human one. His charge had four legs and a wagging tail, button ears, and black eyes sparkling with mischief.

"I wish I could keep from worrying, but you have yet to meet my brothers, Charles and Gareth. You may have won Andrew over, and Lucien too when he crossed the Atlantic to bring me home, but I fear you'll have a harder time of it with the other two, especially Charles."

Ruaidri shrugged, laughing as the puppy licked at his face. "Well then, I hope when they see ye smiling and happy, a babe in your arms and a bloom in yer cheek, they'll forgive me for all of it."

"Gareth will. I'm not so sure about Charles. We were close, and he was always so protective of me."

"And Lucien wasn't?"

She caught his gaze across the short space that separated them, the twinkle in his eye and the easy confidence he was trying so hard to instill in her. Truly, he had a lot more to be concerned about than she did. But that knowledge did nothing to settle her nerves. Lucien and Sir Roger may have cleared her name, and while she may not be exactly lauded back in England at least she wouldn't be hanged as a traitor.

Ruaidri, though, was another matter entirely. She was far more concerned about his safety than she could ever be, her own.

Overhead, clouds moved to cover the sun, and the coach grew momentarily dark. A few drops of rain spluttered against the window, began to roll down the glass. Nerissa opened it despite the weather, hungry for her first scent of home. Of the chalk mud and green grasses, the meadows and dampness and sweet, sweet wind. On the box, the driver called something to his team, and Nerissa moved from her seat, joined her husband on his, and snuggling close to him, leaned her head against his shoulder. His arm came around her, drawing both her and Aidan against him, and she felt his lips in her hair.

"'Tis brave you are for coming back, my love," he murmured. "I know ye're worried."

She spread her hand over his chest, feeling the warmth of his body beneath her cheek, the thump of his heart beneath her palm, the child nestled between them.

"I'm afraid things will be changed. Different from what they used to be."

"Of course, they'll be different. Nothing ever stays the same, Nerissa."

Her unease grew.

More clouds coming in from the west now, following them, slowly overtaking them, and the first splatters of rain against the dust-streaked window.

"And I hope the children will like the puppy."

"Aw, now, lass, who doesn't like a puppy?" His free hand stroked the terrier's head. "Especially this one. Cute as he can be. He'll win hearts, he will."

"He's a little devil."

"Lad's got spirit."

"Maybe we should've kept him ... let him be your ship's dog or something."

"A warship is no place for a dog, Nerissa."

She shrugged. "No place for a cat, either, but everyone seems to have one."

"Cats kill rats."

"So do terriers," she shot back, grinning.

"Aye, well, ye have me there."

"Even if he's a nuisance, I'm sure Celsie will adore this little hooligan. She loves dogs."

"Everyone will love him. You just watch."

She snuggled closer to Ruaidri. The rain was coming down harder now, the grassy chalk downs beyond the window cloaked in mist and almost grey in the shadows.

At last, they were descending into the familiar village of Ravenscombe. Passing the Speckled Hen and the villagers' cottages, the market area, the statue of King Henry on his charger that Gareth and his friends had defaced so long ago. She put a hand against the window, smiling. Remembering. Anticipation outweighing anxiety, excitement pushing aside her worries. Familiar territory, now, and memories everywhere. Shortly, around another bend in the road, Ruaidri, who had once hated all things English and for good reason, would get his first glimpse of Blackheath Castle dominating the countryside, Lucien's pennant undulating against the English sky. Soon, they'd be rolling up to the massive iron-banded doors, she the disgraced daughter of one of England's most aristocratic families, he a rogue Irishman whom most of the nobility would rather spit upon and with them, a baby and a puppy who had a history of making trouble.

Nerissa shuddered.

What could possibly go wrong?

Chapter Two

The weather had been inclement for most of the day, the moody turbulence of spring not quite ready to yield the stage to summer's abundance of warmth and light. Showers had moved in on this late afternoon, and inside the great dining hall of Blackheath Castle, the family had gathered for tea. Ornate plasterwork and Italian art lent the room a rich elegance and on the walls, portraits of de Montforte ancestors gazed down at their living descendants. Steam rose from teacups of finest porcelain. Lit tapers of beeswax glinted off crystal, china, and silver and glowed warmly against the faces of the family, all of them hoping that today would be the day they'd finally get to welcome home a sister, and for most of them, to get their first look at a dubious and still-to-be-approved brother-in-law.

They were an attractive group, the men handsome, athletic, and well-bred, elegant in their frock coats and embroidered waistcoats, the women in beautiful gowns of silk, their hair upswept, their necks, wrists, and fingers adorned with jewels and pearls.

Lucien, the powerful Duke of Blackheath at the head of the table, his wife, Eva, at the foot. Lord Charles, the second eldest of the family, tall and blond, a military man who was not in uniform but whose demeanor was no less the taciturn for it. His beautiful American wife, Amy, so large with child she was uncomfortable in her chair no matter what position she adopted and trying hard not to call attention to the fact. Lord Andrew, his auburn hair drawn back in a loose queue, idly plucking at a slice of lemon cake while his wife, Celsiana, crusader for the plight of abused dogs (and horses), discreetly slipped a biscuit to Esmerelda, who was begging beneath the table. Lord Gareth, a Member of Parliament, who along with his American wife, Juliet, and their two children, had journeyed from his estate in Abingdon to be here for this homecoming that could not, would not, be missed. Even the liveried footmen stationed in the shadows veiled their excitement behind stoic expressions that belied the delight that electrified Blackheath's vast number of servants. Lady Nerissa would arrive any day. It had been, after all, over a year and a half since his Grace's only sister had last been here in her ancestral home.

"Half-five and they're still not here," Celsie lamented. "I guess today won't be the day."

Gareth glanced at the ornate clock on the mantelpiece before directing his gaze out the window into the rainy afternoon. "Don't assume anything. *The Flying White* is probably running late."

"That stage is always running late," Eva affirmed, reaching for her teacup.

Juliet nodded. "It wouldn't know the meaning of the word, *punctual*."

Celsie slipped another piece of biscuit to the setter, hoping no one would notice and knowing that nobody would care, even if they did.

"Maybe they'll be on it," Andrew said hopefully.

"Oh, wouldn't that be nice!" Celsie touched Amy's wrist. "Just in time for your birthday tomorrow!"

"Do you think so? Why, I couldn't wish for a nicer gift."

Juliet raised a speculative brow as she noted how far back from the table poor Amy was seated in order to accommodate her burgeoning belly. "I must say, I wonder if your birthday and the next de Montforte's will end up being one and the same."

"Oh no, the baby isn't due until next month," Amy said, laughing. "We'll keep our own separate birthdays, I think."

The other three women just exchanged glances.

Amy pushed aside her plate. "In any case, I do hope Nerissa has adjusted to life in America as well as I've done in England ... I can't wait to see her, to meet her family, to hear all about everyone back in my old hometown."

Celsie sipped her tea. "I wonder who our little nephew, Aidan, looks like?"

"Nerissa writes that he favors his father," Juliet said. "A head full of curly dark hair but with her eyes."

"I look forward to making the man's acquaintance," Gareth said. He looked at the duke and grinned. "You have the advantage over us, Lucien. You too, Andrew, as you've both met him."

"I'm sure you'll find him quite engaging," Lucien murmured. "Though I daresay he may feel quite ... overwhelmed by the grandeur of this house. Please, all of you, do endeavor to put him at ease. I do not wish him to feel uncomfortable here."

Charles looked into his tea with a flat expression and didn't say a word.

"What do you think he's like?" Celsiana asked breathlessly, looking around the table.

Juliet reached for the sugar. "I never met him myself, but he was the talk of the town back in '75 when he was the Irish Pirate. A dashing smuggler with a bounty on his head. If it wasn't for him, I think it's safe to say many people in Boston would've starved under the blockade. He made sure food got through. And arms." She smiled, remembering. "He sure was a thorn in the Royal Navy's side, but to Boston, he was a hero."

"Oh, my," said Celsie, fascinated. "Amy, did you ever meet him?"

"I'm afraid not." She smiled. "But I'm told he's very handsome."

Charles's expression went even flatter, and he picked up his teacup, staring into space as he took a sip.

"I fear I'll never be able to wrap my tongue around his name," Celsie lamented, turning to her husband. "Andrew, can you pronounce it for us all again?"

"Roo-a-ree. And he's not the sort to take offense if you don't get it right."

"All the same, it would be quite rude not to at least try."

"Roo-a-ree," Andrew repeated.

"Rory?" Celsie tried, hopefully.

Laughter, and a ripple of nervous excitement.

"Maybe I should just stick to Captain O'Devir," Celsie murmured. "Unless that is dreadfully formal."

Charles pushed away his teacup.

"What is it, Charles?" Amy's hand went to her husband's. "Did you meet him when you served in Boston?"

"Thankfully not."

"Charles!"

"Forgive me if I cannot share in the excitement," he said sharply. "That blackguard has a long way to go before I can forgive what he did."

Glances were exchanged in the sudden uncomfortable silence and Gareth cleared his throat. But it was Amy, her dark brown eyes suddenly sad, who squeezed her husband's fingers. "I know this is hard for you, but please, just give him a chance," she said softly.

"As if he deserves one!"

The duke's black gaze swung wordlessly to his

brother. Charles met it with defiance. It was during this tense moment they suddenly all heard it. Hoofbeats. The sound of wheels on the crushed stone outside. A yapping dog. Voices.

"Ohhhh!"

"Is that them?"

"Well, who else would it be?"

Hopeful glances were exchanged, and unable to help herself, Celsie jumped up from her chair and hurried to the window.

"They're here!" she squealed.

Excitement rippled around the table, the women tittering and the men grinning. Charles took a sip of his tea and remained unmoving, his stare directed at the opposite wall. Andrew regarded him and exchanged a worried glance with Lucien. Esmerelda scooted from beneath the table and out of the room, and a moment later, her frenzied barking could be heard out in the Great Hall. Celsie rushed back to her chair and quickly smoothed her skirts.

"Ohh!" Amy said happily, taking Juliet's hand in excitement.

"Should we rush to greet them or stay here and pretend a measure of civilized aplomb?" Gareth asked, looking around the table.

"Let's stay here," Eva said. "It sounds as though Esmerelda's already overwhelming them with delight at seeing her long-lost mistress. No need to add to it. They'll be tired after such a long journey, and will wish to come in, sit down, and have some refreshment."

"Judging by Esmerelda's bark, she must approve of him!" Celsie exclaimed.

"She's a setter," Charles muttered. "She approves of everyone."

Celsie pretended she hadn't heard. "I bet he's a dog lover!"

"Ohh, here they come!"

Out in the hall beyond the doors, they heard foot-steps and approaching voices: Nerissa's excited chatter, a man's deep murmur, a small dog yapping in excitement, and Esmerelda's happy barks, woofs and whines.

"By God, I've missed that laugh of hers," said Gareth, grinning. "She sounds so happy."

"Because she *is* happy," Lucien murmured with a warning look at Charles. "And you, my brother, will do nothing to make her regret bringing the man she loves here. You will treat him with civility and respect no matter what your feelings. Do you understand?"

"You ask a lot of me," the major snapped. "I have no wish to—"

"That's enough," Lucien said firmly. "You cannot pass judgment on him until you've met him."

"I've no need to meet him, I have no desire to meet him—"

"You will treat him as one of the family," Lucien warned.

"You would take his side over your own brother's?"

"There are no *sides* here. Your sister has made her choice, just as you did, just as you all did. You will re-spect that."

"Well, some of us didn't have a choice," Celsie quipped, trying to lighten the rising tension.

"Isn't that the truth," Gareth added.

Amy placed a hand on her husband's arm. "Just give him a chance, Charles. That's all that is asked of you."

Charles's handsome face darkened.

Outside the doors, somewhere out in the hall, the voices grew louder as the newcomers approached.

Lucien leaned forward, his eyes hard with warning. "He has made our sister happy. She loves him deeply. He has given her a life of joy, adventure, and purpose. He deserves our gratitude."

"That's not what you were saying when you charged

off across the Atlantic to bring her back after he stole her right out from under Andrew's nose!"

"The circumstances were ... different."

"You went over there intending to kill him in cold blood!"

"Indeed, I tried. But you will note I did not succeed, nor did I bring him—or our sister—back. Their union and contentment satisfied me as the head of this family, Charles, and you will let it be enough for you as well."

Charles gripped the edge of the table with both hands, leaned forward, and finally lost his temper. "Has everyone forgotten he *abducted* her!"

Horrified gasps, shocked faces, one or two hands clapped to a mouth, and Amy reaching out to lay a soothing hand on his wrist just as two people appeared at the open doors, Esmerelda's long feathered tail thumping against their legs.

The tall, confident man displayed a natural charisma, with the commanding stance of a leader and eyes that weren't quite blue and weren't quite violet but something in between. His lean angular face and high cheekbones contrasted with wildly curling black hair caught neatly at his nape. He held a puppy in his arms whose tail whipped against the buttons of his fine green coat. If the opulence of his surroundings made him uncomfortable, he didn't show it. If he felt intimidated and out of place within this grand and ancient home that had been the seat of some of the bluest blood in England, he gave no hint of it. And if he'd heard Charles's outburst—which surely he had—he was choosing to ignore it.

Nerissa, there at his side, was choosing *not* to ignore it. She held a fussing child in her arms, and her pale blue eyes were hurt and accusing as she turned them on Charles.

"Well, that is not *quite* the homecoming I'd envisioned," she said icily. "Perhaps it was a mistake to come here."

"Easy now, *mo grá,*" her husband murmured in a startling thick Irish accent. "Just let it go."

Charles slammed down his napkin and began to stand up.

It was Lucien who smoothly took control of the situation. Rising, he came around the table, warmly exchanged bows with the Irishman, and embraced his sister as the rest of the family, looking on, held their breaths in horrified anticipation.

"Ah, my dear, dear Nerissa ... Ruaidri ... how very *good* it is to see you both again. You must tell us all about your trip. And may I?" He reached out to take the child from his sister. She cast a final accusatory look at Charles and then turned her back on him without further ado. "You must be Aidan, our newest little nephew. Hello, young fellow!" Pulling back the child's knit cap so his face could be more easily seen, the duke angled him toward his family while guiding Nerissa and her husband—still carrying the squirming puppy—to their chairs. "Welcome to Blackheath. Shall we make the introductions?"

Chapter Three

"And let's start with the puppy!" cried Celsie, clapping her hands in glee, perhaps with a bit more enthusiasm than the situation warranted. Like the others, she was keen to defuse the tension before things could go from bad to worse. "Oh, where did you both find such a sweet little dog?"

But the de Montforte brothers had risen to their feet and her words were all but lost in the clamor as introductions were made, laughter exchanged, complements were swapped and welfare inquired about.

"Nerissa, you look radiant!" gushed Amy. "American life must favor you!"

Embraces, more smiles, the child in Lucien's arms yawning and a young nurse— quietly summoned from upstairs—swooping in to take the child up to the nursery.

Throughout it all, the puppy's yapping continued.

The Irishman looked to Nerissa, uncertain what he should do with the squirming bundle.

"Just set him down, Ruaidri," she said. "We don't stand on any ceremony here when it comes to family pets."

"Are ye certain that's such a good idea?"

"He'll be fine," Celsie assured him.

He put the puppy down. The terrier immediately shot beneath the table and seized the rug, rump raised, front paws outstretched, and tail whipping, his eyes naughty as his teeth worried the ancient Persian carpet. Celsie reached down and grabbed him. The puppy refused to let go of his prize until she finally pried open his jaws and lifted him to her lap. Esmerelda was also under the table, nose now firmly planted in the puppy's bottom. The puppy reared up on his hind legs and rotated his head like a windmill, paws flying, squealing in excitement as he tried to get down to play with the older dog. Celsie finally relented and lowered him to the floor once more and the two shot out of the room in a skitter of toenails and yapping.

"What is his name?" Eva inquired. "He certainly seems to have ... energy."

Nerissa allowed Ruaidri to seat her. "He doesn't yet have one. We thought the children might like to name him." In response to the questioning looks, she added, "He's a gift. From America."

"Aye, one of our neighbors had a litter. The little devil's mother is the best ratter he's ever had," said the captain as he took his own chair. "Not implyin', o' course, that ye have rats," he added hastily.

"My dear Ruaidri," Lucien intoned. "I'm sure there are rats aplenty out where the chickens are penned, if not in the stables themselves. Doubtless he will have much to keep him occupied."

The Irishman's smile was quick, relieved, and Charles, discreetly watching him, saw that despite his initial confidence O'Devir was indeed uncomfortable and feeling very much out of place here in this grand ancestral home that was chalk and cheese from the quaint fishing village in Connemara where he'd grown up.

He returned his attention to his tea, gazing into the

depths of his cup while his family did their best to welcome the man.

You don't belong here.

He lifted the cup to his lips, the scalding brew on his tongue punctuating his thoughts.

You're not good enough for my sister, you thieving wretch.

And Lucien, also trying to put the rogue at ease. The others, trying to smooth the way for him so he wouldn't feel awkward and out of place.

After what he did to Nerissa, Charles thought bitterly, with a discreet glance at his little sister. She was happily babbling about the voyage and all but ignoring him. *After what you did to this family.* He studied her with a critical eye. Searched her face, her voice, her very form for the least shadow of unhappiness, despair, abuse, anything that would justify his preconceived feelings about this ... this knave that she had married.

He found nothing.

And felt Lucien's gaze heavy on his.

He glanced over. His brother just gave a faintly perceptible nod, and something churned in Charles's gut.

Don't be rude, his brother's black eyes warned.

"Well, you said you'd be here by the time the roses were in bloom," he heard himself saying to his sister, who turned frosty blue eyes upon him. "You timed it well. Mama's flowers are just beginning to open near the gatehouse."

"Ruaidri promised he'd get me here in time to see them, and he did."

Charles forced a thin smile, wondering if Ireland had gained a new saint named Ruaidri to go along with their Patrick and Brendan.

The Irishman recognized Charles's attempt to join the conversation. "Nerissa tells me ye were stationed in Boston back in '75?"

"Yes."

"Which regiment?"

"Fourth foot. King's own."

Charles abruptly reached for his cup. He had no wish to exchange pleasantries with the man and made no attempt to hide the fact. Again, he felt Lucien's dark, warning gaze upon him. He sipped his tea, and a glance at his wife only added to his irritation. Amy was staring at O'Devir in awe, and Juliet and Celsiana were twittering like fledgling titmice. Charles felt his pulse getting louder in his ears. A vein pounding in his temple. And now Gareth was saying something about it being too bad that Charles and Ruaidri hadn't met back then in Boston, Charles was privately thanking God they had not, and Eva, making small talk and showing proper interest as hostess, was discreetly studying the newcomer behind a welcoming smile. Her catlike green gaze went to Charles's. Was the Duchess of Blackheath sharing his thoughts? Did she, too, wonder what Nerissa had found so intriguing in such a rough, ill-bred man?

A pirate. A thief. A hero to the New England colonies, who'd been handpicked (or so Andrew said) by John Adams for the special mission that had crossed his path with Nerissa's, who was supposedly now some prominent officer in the American Navy. They must be really scraping the bottom of the barrel, Charles decided, if common thieves were elevated to such ranks.

You are being churlish.

His conscience all but yelled the words at him.

And his family's pleas. *Give the man a chance.*

"So how was your crossing?" Eva asked, pouring herself another cup of tea.

"Uneventful," Nerissa said happily. "Nobody harassed us, chased us, or tried to apprehend us, though Ruaidri is far too clever to ever get caught. Oh, and we did run into a squall just east of Newfoundland. It was most dreadful, with large swells that would've swept anyone overboard who wasn't roped to something strong, but Ruaidri kept us all safe and the ship too. I was never worried."

"Ah, lass, you give me credit when it should go to the good Lord above," O'Devir said, reaching for his own tea. Charles noted the hand he extended was large, calloused and scarred, deeply tanned from years at sea. It was a working man's hand, and it looked strangely out of place against the elegant porcelain of the cup.

"Even so, if it weren't for your skills, I'm not sure we'd all be sitting here talking about it."

"'Wasn't such a big storm as all that, lass."

"Well, it was the biggest one I've ever seen and if I never experience another like it, I'll count myself most fortunate."

"Did you get seasick?" Gareth asked.

"Oh, no. I have never been seasick. Ruaidri says I make the perfect sailor's wife."

Ruaidri this, Ruaidri that, God help me. Charles began to wonder how he could extricate both himself and Amy from this dreadful gathering and call it an early—a very early—night, without appearing any ruder than he'd already shown himself to be.

"Do you have a big ship?" Celsie asked, sneaking a bit of cake to the dog at her feet. "One from the American Navy?"

Nerissa exchanged a grin with her husband. "Oh, gosh, no. That would hardly do, now, would it? Captain Merrick and his wife, Mira, offered to bring us in their schooner, but Ruaidri took a smart little sloop as a prize some time back, and we renamed her and took her instead. She is quite seaworthy, is she not, Ruaidri?"

"She is indeed, lass."

"Isn't it bad luck to rename a ship?" Charles managed tightly.

"The Royal Navy does so all the time," Nerissa retorted, and Charles heard the sharpness in her tone behind the blithe delivery of her words. "If it's good enough for them, it's good enough for us."

Us.

So now she called herself an American, and not an Englishwoman?

She, who was the only daughter of one of the oldest, most prominent families in England?

He looked down, veiling his expression, determined not to make a scene or spoil his sister's homecoming, despite how much her words burned him, no matter how much it felt as though she was baiting him with her praise of Saint Ruaidri's godlike qualities. She was no longer the little sister with whom he'd always been so close. She was no longer the Nerissa he'd always known and loved; she was this rogue's wife. She was changed, different, almost unrecognizable, and it was obvious where her loyalties lay.

It pained him.

Angered him.

She could have done better. So much better.

Why hadn't she?

And now she was happily reaching for her tea, her gaze meeting her husband's over the rim of her teacup, full of adoration and a worship that Charles found sickening.

"In any case, the crossing was rather uneventful, and despite the fact we were buffeted by the storm, we all came through just fine. Even little Aidan never got fearful or sick. He must have inherited Ruaidri's seafaring blood."

Charles rubbed his forehead and resisted the urge to look at the mantelpiece clock.

Lucien wiped his mouth with his napkin. "And how are Captain Merrick and his wife, Mira?"

"They are quite well. They send their regards, of course."

"I miss Mira," Amy put in, referring to her old

friend back in Newburyport. "We write to each other, of course, but it's not the same."

"Well, I confess it took me some time to warm up to her—I mean, she is quite unconventional, and says the most shocking things!—but we've developed a warm friendship and she always goes out of her way to help me with things that I'm still getting used to. It is a different life there. If it weren't for her, I'd be so dreadfully homesick. But she keeps me laughing."

Amy looked down at her plate. "And my ... family? The Leightons?"

"Your brother, Will, has a sweetheart, your father has been courting a widow in the church, and those two stepsisters of yours are still unmarried."

"Probably always will be," Charles said beneath his breath, remembering the evil the two young women had visited upon him, but those were memories that were in the past and he willfully returned them to their rightful place.

Lucien leaned back in his chair. "Perhaps for the next reunion, we will all come to you, instead of you having to come all the way to England. I should like to see your new home, Nerissa, under less trying circumstances than I left it."

"Hear, hear!"

"A toast to Newburyport," Gareth said merrily, raising his glass. "This place that I've yet to see but which I've heard so much about. If it makes you happy, sweet sister, then it makes me happy to come visit. Fancy a trip across the great blue sea, Juliet?"

"It's not one I ever thought to make again, but I would love to see Nerissa's new home."

And so the tension of the initial meeting softened, to become a soft thrum beneath the bright smiles, chatter, laughter and dogs that returned to wrestle and play beneath the table, until a furry back hit one of the table legs, a cup overturned, and Nerissa, scooping up the puppy, declared she was exhausted and wanted nothing more than to sleep in her old bed.

"You both must be tired from such a long journey," Celsie said, reaching for the puppy. "Why don't you let Andrew and I take him tonight. Is he housebroken?"

"Well…"

"He'll sleep in the bed with us until we all figure out where and with whom he'll reside. Andrew? Are you good with another dog in the bed?"

He shut his eyes and made a helpless little motion with his hand. "Of course, Celsie. What's one more dog."

"Well, this one is small, and he'll be no trouble." She laughed as the puppy licked her face. "Will you, little one? Perhaps tomorrow when the children are all here, they'll come up with a proper name for you."

They all rose from the table, goodnights were exchanged along with yawns and vows to see each other at supper, and as they did so, Nerissa found a moment to press close to Charles, who felt stung, confused, and adrift in feelings he didn't understand.

She leaned closer, her words meant for him alone.

"Give him a chance, Charles. I know it's hard. But I beg of you, just try."

And then she stood on tiptoe, gave him a kiss on the cheek, and taking her husband's arm, led him out of the room.

Chapter Four

Her apartments were exactly as she'd last seen and remembered them, though the bedroom itself seemed more grand, more pretentious, more exaggerated, and a bit too over the top compared to what she'd become accustomed to in her new home across the sea.

They had put little Aidan in a bassinet near the hearth, where Ruaidri read him a story that he invented as it came to him, until the child was fisting his eyes and yawning. Eventually, he fell asleep. Holding hands, his mother and father watched him for a long moment, then each leaned down to kiss his soft curls. Nerissa pulled a blanket up over his tiny shoulders and then turned toward the bed.

"I know it's early, but I do feel the need to rest. Perhaps we should take the evening meal on trays and make our appearances at breakfast instead."

"Whatever suits ye best, lass."

She stood there, looking at her old bed in the rich, warm candlelight.

The silver and blue hangings, once so richly sumptuous, now seemed extravagant. The gilt this, the gilt that, felt overdone. Excessive. The high ceilings and ornate plasterwork seemed almost gaudy. Nerissa spread her hand across the coverlet, thinking.

Ruaidri came up to her. "Are y' well, lass?"

"It feels different, now," she said a bit wistfully. "When I last slept in this bed, I was a girl who believed she was a woman. A bird in a gilded cage, who thought her life was mapped out for her, who was meant to marry a man she'd known since she was a child. A girl who took all that for granted. Now ... I return as someone very different. I return as a wife, as a mother ... all grown up, now. And I don't feel as if I quite belong here anymore, if that makes sense."

"Ye'll always belong here, *mo grá*. 'Tis your childhood home."

"Yes." She turned and went into his arms, laying her cheek against his heart. "And that's just it, is it not? *Childhood* home. But I'm not the same person I was when I left here all those months ago, Ruaidri. I'm different. Changed."

"We all get older and wiser. And none of us can go back to our childhoods."

"And I anticipated a better homecoming. Things felt so very awkward down there. What did I subject you to? I don't know what I was thinking."

His hard-calloused fingers stroked the back of her neck, pulled out one of the long pins that held her thick ivory hair in its elaborate coif. "It actually went better than I thought it would," he confessed.

"Really?"

"Well, think of it. Gareth and Charles have never met me. To them, I'm an evil pile of shite who took their little sister away, forever and for good. They have good reason to despise me, as I would them if the situation was reversed."

"It's not Gareth I'm worried about. It's Charles."

"Ah, love. Maybe when he realizes how happy you are, he'll come around."

She shrugged, remembering the cold hurt in her brother's pale blue eyes, his barely contained anger. "I don't know, Ruaidri. But even if he does not, it doesn't change things between us. You are my husband. I love you with my whole heart, my entire being. You know that, don't you?"

"Of course, I do."

"And I know how hard it must be for you to keep your own temper in the face of such ill treatment ... such insults." She closed her eyes, her lashes fluttering against his shirt. "I wish we had never come here."

"Here now, Sunshine. Give it time. We only just arrived."

"I know, but if Charles doesn't come around—"

"If ye're worried that yer brother and I'll get into a duel, rest assured I won't let that happen. I tangled once, and only once, with Lucien. I've no taste for going at it with yet another brother."

That got a smile out of her, as he intended it would, and she felt herself relax, just a bit. She stood there, enclosed within the protective circle of his arms, his heartbeat steady and reassuring beneath her ear. He was here, he was holding her, he was her life now, along with Aidan. It didn't matter if she had grown in ways that made her feel almost like a stranger here, now. It didn't matter that it was raining outside and growing dark, that she felt suddenly homesick for Newburyport, that the wonderful homecoming she had imagined had been a fantasy, that she just wanted to cry. Nothing mattered, except the feel of her husband's strong arms around her. It would be all right. With Ruaidri, it was always all right.

She listened to the rain beating against the ancient leaded windows, a sound she had known for all of her life.

Home.
England.
Ruaidri.

"Do you think they liked the puppy?" she ventured, after some time.

She felt his lips in her hair. "Well now, who doesn't like a puppy, eh?"

"This one is such a little scamp ... so much energy, and he's devious."

"Aren't all puppies? He'll be a good dog, someday."

"Someday," she agreed, dubiously. "I hope that when the children meet him tomorrow, they'll have a good name for him. He's been cooped up for a month ... aboard the ship, aboard the coach ... maybe after he gets some exercise, he'll settle down."

Ruaidri laughed.

"Well, we can hope!"

"No matter what, he'll liven this place up. And I'm sure the little ones'll love him. They'll tire each other out. Children and dogs ... doesn't get better than that."

She stood there within the circle of his arms, listening to the rain outside. The fire snapping in the hearth, the deep stillness all around her in the thickening gloom. As bad as things had been tonight, perhaps things would be better in the morning after they'd had a proper night's sleep. A fresh start. God knew, they all needed one.

He spoke her thoughts, as he so often did. "Tomorrow's another day, Nerissa."

"Yes, Ruaidri. Another day."

"And it'll be a good day. We'll make it so."

She pulled back and looked up at him. He smiled down at her, a solid, steady presence, reassuring, optimistic. She would never get tired of looking at his arresting face with its arching brows, bold nose, and hard angles. The violet eyes that were fringed with long lashes, warming now in unspoken invitation.

"An early bedtime, *mo grá?*"

"I thought you'd never ask." She pressed close,

lifting her face to his as she sought his lips. "Undress me, my dear husband."

But his hands were already working their magic.

❧

SEVERAL HOURS later and a few doors away, Celsie and Andrew were also in bed. Unlike the new arrivals, they weren't asleep.

And it looked as if that desired state might elude them this night unless drastic changes were made to their sleeping arrangements.

Or rather, the sleeping arrangements of the puppy.

"This wasn't a good idea," Andrew grumbled, his body already contorted at an unnatural angle to accommodate Esmerelda curled up against the back of his legs, a small white turnspit named Moll who had insinuated herself between himself and Celsie, much to his lament, and now the puppy, who seemed to possess the energy of a racehorse pumped up on oats. Or a child who'd imbibed too much sugar. On a floor cushion on his side of the bed, the fat and aging bulldog, Pork, was already snoring and farting up a storm. Clouds of gas wafted up, more potent than normal, and Andrew felt his lungs seize up in protest.

He yanked the sheet up and buried his nose in it, trying to filter the air so he could breathe.

"He'll settle down," Celsie said dubiously as the puppy sprang out of her embrace, jumped onto Esmerelda in an attempt to get her to play, received a warning growl to back off, and then leaped off the bed and promptly began sniffing the floor.

"Tell me again why he's in here with us?"

She climbed out of the bed and grabbed him before he could squat. The puppy squirmed in her arms and licked her chin. "Well, where else is he supposed to stay? It wouldn't be fair to poor Nerissa and Ruaidri to take him after such a long trip. They're probably exhausted and need sleep."

"I need sleep too. Besides, this bed isn't big enough for two people and now three dogs."

"What's one more? Besides, he's little. He won't take up much room."

"He could stay in the kennel like a proper dog."

"A little puppy? In a kennel? Oh, Andrew, how *could* you..."

He rolled his eyes, knowing it was a losing battle when it came to dogs. "Well, neither one of us are going to get any rest—"

"He'll settle down once we blow out the candle," Celsie assured him. "Even puppies need to sleep."

"This one doesn't look ready, willing, or able to sleep. How do we know what he's going to get into once we both drop off? I think I should go hunt down a box of some sort to put him in for the night and bring him down to the kitchens."

"He'll howl up a storm and keep everyone awake."

"I'm sure he will."

"And *I'm* sure that with some time and training, he'll be a very good little dog." She kissed the puppy's head and then gazed deeply into his black button eyes. "Won't you, little angel?"

"Little hooligan, more like."

"He's a terrier. He can't help that he's got energy."

Andrew just rubbed his eyes, the need to sleep weighing on him.

Celsie didn't look any more tired than the puppy in her arms. "I can't wait until tomorrow. To get all the children together, to get to know our new brother-in-law ... their little boy favors him, don't you think? And doesn't he just adore Nerissa! The way he looks at her! I'm so glad things didn't work out with her and Perry and that Ruaidri came along when he did. They were meant for each other, don't you think?"

"I wasn't convinced at first, but as I've come to know the fellow, yes, I agree. They are very well suited. I just hope Charles comes around."

"Well, as you've said, Charles and Nerissa were always close ... and unlike you and Lucien, he has not had the chance to get to know Ruaidri. I have faith he'll eventually accept him. Besides, he's probably worried about Amy and the coming child, and the stress of that can't be helping things any."

Andrew stifled a yawn. "I'm sure you are right, my dear."

"We'll throw a party for Amy's birthday. That should help put Charles in better spirits."

Andrew nodded and rubbed his eyes again. "Let's hope."

"Children, dogs, and a birthday party. So much to look forward to! We should try to get some sleep, Andrew. Oh, puppy! You're going to have to settle down. Do you need to go outside one last time?"

"I'll take him out," Andrew said, getting out of bed, donning his robe, and reaching for the terrier.

"Thank you, Andrew." She smiled a bit apologetically as she handed the squirming dog over. "We'll both sleep better knowing his bladder is empty before we blow out the candle."

"You and I both know that neither of us are going to sleep tonight."

A soft *pfffffitttt* issued from the back end of the bulldog, still snoring on his bed on the floor, and Andrew pinched his nostrils shut and breathed through his mouth. "What in God's name has Lucien been feeding that dog?"

Celsie's mouth twitched with humor.

"Right, I'll be back shortly. Keep my side of the bed warm." He gave a rueful glance at Esmerelda, who had stretched and expanded to claim the space where he had just lain. "If you can get to it."

"You are an angel, Andrew."

Pffffftttt. "Trust me, I just want some fresh air."

Celsie crawled into bed, slid Esmerelda's heavy weight over so Andrew would have room when he came back, and moved Moll over as well. It would be tight quarters tonight with her and Andrew sleeping board-to-board to accommodate the dogs, but she didn't mind, as a crowded bed meant she was all the closer to her husband.

She lay in the bed, looking up at the hangings and counting her blessings.

A handsome, intelligent, loving man who put up with her dogs. Life was good.

Chapter Five

❧

D awn.
The first rays of sunshine touched the downs, and mist clung to the vale in which the village of Ravenscombe was nestled. A chill was still in the air, and in the great kitchens downstairs, servants were lighting the fire and beginning to prepare breakfast.

Not long afterward, the family itself went about rising.

Lucien, grateful, relieved, and even excited that his family was together again at last, had slept peacefully in his tower bedroom, his duchess in his arms.

Gareth and Juliet had also slept well, as had Charles (after lying awake in the darkness for a long time, battling his conflicting emotions over his new brother-in-law) and Amy. Nerissa, safe in her husband's arms, had passed the night in deep, dreamless slumber, though Ruaidri had been somewhat restless in the great chamber in which his wife had grown up, finding it stuffy, oppressive, and overdone.

Andrew and Celsie had not slept at all.

They came down to breakfast, bleary eyed, pale, and holding the puppy which, Lucien decided after taking one look at the little dog, was the likely reason for their fatigued appearance this morning.

"Sleep well?" he asked innocently as he took his seat at the head of the table.

Andrew just glared at him while Celsie suppressed a smirk.

The doors opened and Gareth appeared along with Juliet. "Morning, everyone!"

"Good morning."

"Anyone fancy a ride out over the downs after breakfast?"

"A ride or a race?"

"Right, let's make it a race."

Lucien reached for a roll. He buttered it and then put it on Eva's plate. "I think Eva and I are going to walk out and inspect some of the fencing in the east pasture," he said. "Why don't you see if you can interest Ruaidri in going?" He glanced toward the door. "I think it would be good to try to integrate him into the family... Make him feel welcome."

"Does he ride?" Gareth asked.

"Why wouldn't he?"

Gareth shrugged. "Most mariners don't seem as comfortable on the back of a horse as they do the deck of a ship."

"I daresay there is nothing ... typical, about your new brother," Lucien drawled, reaching for coffee. "But if you're going out for a ride, I suggest you also invite Charles. It would be a good opportunity for him to get to know our captain."

"I have little wish to get to know him."

"Ah, Charles." Lucien smiled up at his brother, who stood in the doorway with Amy. "I daresay it's not like you to be so churlish. Did you not sleep well?"

"I slept fine."

"You must give Ruaidri a chance. As Andrew did, and as I did."

"Just because the two of you think he's the patron

saint of Ireland doesn't mean I'm obligated to share your feelings."

"Charles," Amy said, taking his arm. "Lucien's right. If you alienate him, you'll alienate Nerissa as well. Is that what you wish?"

Charles sighed and took a seat. "I really cannot stomach being under the same roof as that blackguard. And I can't pretend an affection for him that I do not feel."

"Ahem."

There in the doorway stood the subject of his ire, with Nerissa, their child in her arms, alongside him. The man took a deep breath and offered a nod of greet-ing, which Charles did not return. He looked at his sister instead. Her eyes were bleak. Angry. Hurt.

"Charles, must you be so very odious? So rude?"

He flushed hotly. He could not hold his sister's gaze, and instead, reached for a piece of fruit. The air crackled with awkwardness, and he didn't say a word as the two newcomers took their seats.

It was the Irishman who broke the tension. "Fine pile ye got here, Blackheath," he said jovially. "What do you do around here to amuse yerself, eh?"

"Manipulate people," Celsie said with false in-nocence.

The duke smiled and shook his head. "Those days are past, my dear. You're all happily married, now. My work is done. No more schemes." He took a long sip of his coffee and his black gaze settled on Ruaidri. "To an-swer your question, though ... I begin my day with a long walk before the sun is fully risen—good for both the dogs and me, I daresay—attend to various orders of business both domestic and political, enjoy breakfast and then take Armageddon out for a gallop."

"That's it?"

"Country life is rather dull, I'm afraid."

"Not half as exciting as blowing up ships and

fighting wars," Andrew added as an aside to Ruaidri. "I hope you won't be bored."

"Bored?" The Irishman waited as a footman poured coffee for him, picked up the cup, and took a long swallow. He set it down, smiling with pleasure. "Saints alive, this coffee alone'll make up for any so-called boredom," he said. "The swill my cook makes aboard ship is lamentable."

Everyone laughed except Charles, who pointedly gazed out the window.

"Charles and I often engage in a horse race when we're both home," Gareth offered. "Do you ride? You're welcome to join us."

Nerissa nudged her husband's arm. "You should join them."

"I might." He looked at Andrew, who was rubbing his eyes and stifling a yawn. "Ye going to go, Andrew?"

"No, not today."

"Andrew didn't sleep much last night," Celsie said wryly.

Nerissa looked at them in concern. "Why not?"

"The great unnamed," Andrew muttered, shooting a glance at the puppy on Celsie's lap.

She pulled the little dog close. "You *did* agree to take him into our bed."

"And you came up with the idea, so you can't lay the entire blame on me."

"Aye, he's feisty, that one," Ruaidri agree. "How about we take him tonight? He knows us ... maybe he'll settle down a bit."

"You've had such a long trip. We can take him," Juliet offered. "Right, Gareth?'

"Sure," he said, spreading jam on a roll. "Dogs love me. He'll sleep."

Andrew shook his head. "We'll try him again tonight. If he keeps us awake a second time, one of you lot can have him tomorrow."

A footman brought in another pot of tea. Comments were exchanged about the bright sunny day outside, the state of the ongoing war, and inquiries about the welfare and doings of the next generation of the family.

"And where are all the little ones?" Ruaidri asked. "Seems awfully quiet around here."

"Upstairs in the nursery," Juliet offered. "When we have a large family gathering, they insist on all being together, day and night. Even the youngest of the lot. I know, an English nursery is a bit different from the way we do things in Boston and I daresay, Captain, where you grew up, but the children love it. They play games, make mischief, sleep in pretend-tents and cause their nurses to pull their hair out."

Amy nodded and rested a hand on her belly. "They'll be down shortly."

"Yes, be prepared," Eva said with sparkling eyes.

As if to punctuate her words, there was a sudden cacophony of shrieks, giggles, and yelling, and what sounded like a distant rumble.

"Here they come," said Juliet, and a moment later the doors flew open and the room was full of children, two harried nurses some distance behind them.

"Aunt Nerissa!"

"And oh, look, a puppy!"

The puppy immediately started yapping in Celsie's arms, tail beating against her bodice as he tried to get down to see the children.

Nerissa passed Aidan to her husband and opened her arms as the excited brood ran around the table and tried to pile into her lap, some of them going to the puppy immediately afterward, some staring at Ruaidri. Charlotte, the oldest, blonde and blue-eyed, the only one who had any real memories of the aunt she resembled so much. Not quite six in years, she had a serious nature about her, but was all studied politeness and smiles as she watched each of her cousins swarm her aunt and new uncle.

Nerissa was overwhelmed. How much they had all grown in a year and a half. And how much she had missed—first words and first teeth, first Christmases and first friendships and even first times on a horse. Charlotte, self-appointed little spokesperson of the group. Her brother, Gabriel, his hair a few shades darker than his sister's, the spark of deviltry that had so defined Gareth already lighting his pale blue eyes. Little Mary, an orange tabby clutched in her arms that was staring balefully at the puppy in Celsie's; she favored her mother, Amy, but her huge dark eyes had the steady, focused observance of her father, Charles, and she had not lost her shy reticence. Tiny Laura, almost three now, with Andrew's dark russet locks and a big smile that grew all the wider when she saw the puppy her mother held, her little brother, Justin, squalling in Nurse's, and now Andrew's, arms. And finally Augustus, the young Marquess of Ravenscombe and heir apparent to the great Duchy of Blackheath, dark haired, dark-eyed, and quite tall for his age, unmistakably Lucien's son in everything about him from looks to mannerisms.

"Who are you?" he asked of Ruaidri, eyeing him with lordly suspicion.

"This is your uncle, Captain Ruaidri," Eva said kindly. "And I'm sure he will be very happy to regale you all with stories of ships and the sea, mermaids, whales, and the many places to which he has sailed."

"Oh, my!" young Mary breathed, holding her kitten close. "Have you ever seen a sea monster?"

"Well, now, lass, off the coast of Newfoundland a few years back I did once see something that caused me hair to stand on end and—"

"You talk funny," said Gabriel.

"Gabriel!" Juliet scolded. "That is quite rude. You apologize to your uncle."

"Well, he does talk funny," ventured little Laura. "But I would very much like to hear about the sea monster. Please continue, Uncle Ruaidri."

"Roo-a-ree," squealed Gabriel. "Your name is funny too!"

Mary shyly took a step closer. "May we hear about the sea monster, sir?"

Ruaidri O'Devir didn't seem offended in the least, and Charles, watching this exchange, felt his irritation increasing. So, the rogue was now charming his very daughter as well as his wife. Resentment clenched his veins, and he felt a muscle tightening in his jaw.

He rose and pushed back his chair, his breakfast unfinished. "I am going to take that gallop across the downs now," he said tightly. "Gareth?"

"I'm going to sit right here and hear about the sea monster, but I'll be out in ten minutes."

"Suit yourself."

Charles stalked from the room and left them all. He moved through the Great Hall, its vaulted stone ceiling rising high above him, his shoes rapping a tattoo across the polished marble floor, the suits of armor in their wall notches staring sightlessly out at him through slitted visors. He made for the great medieval doors with their banded iron and studded bolts. Pushed them open and moved purposely down the steps. In the stable he found Contender, and too impatient to call for a groom, too annoyed at the world to wait around while someone else got busy with a task he was fully able to complete himself, found the saddle and bridle and carried them back to the stall, hanging them over the partition while he curried the horse. He was so caught up in his anger that he never heard his wife come up behind him until her soft voice cut through the sounds of the brush, briskly flicking the dust from the big chestnut's gleaming coat.

"Charles."

He paused, the brush in his hand, and looked at her. She sounded out of breath. Her face was flushed with the effort of walking out here, and her eyes were both sad and condemning. It fueled his peevishness all the more.

He turned away and kept brushing.

"It is not like you to be so rude," she said quietly. "Why do you despise him so?"

"It is unrealistic to expect a man to get on with every person he meets. There's always going to be someone you don't like, someone who rubs you the wrong way, someone you just don't wish to be around."

"He never did anything to you."

"Would that he had, as I'd find it a damned sight easier to feel charitable toward him had it been me he'd done something to, not Nerissa." The brush moved faster. "He may be some self-styled naval officer now, but when I was stationed in Boston, he was a pirate. A smuggler, a thief, a wanted man with a price on his head. I know more about him than anyone because I knew what his reputation was, Amy, and it wasn't a good one. And you want me to approve of him for my sister? He, who abducts her, marries her, takes her far away from us, and then shows up here expecting us to treat him like one of the family?"

"But he *is* one of the family, whether you like it or not."

"I dislike it intensely."

"I think you should give him a chance. Lucien thinks highly of him, Andrew likes him, and even Gareth is in there laughing at the silly sea-monster story."

"That doesn't mean I have to like him," Charles bit out, stung that Gareth, too, was falling under the rogue's spell.

"It's my birthday. I would like it very much if, for my

sake as well as your sister's, you can at least pretend to be civil."

"It'll be pretense, all right."

Her dark eyes were pleading. "And I hope you can find it in your heart to at least try to make him feel welcome. Soon enough they'll be going back to America and then how will you feel? You'll have missed your chance. And maybe next time, they won't be quite so eager to come back."

Charles said nothing. He tossed the brush aside, picked up the saddle cloth, spread it briskly over the thoroughbred's back, and hefted the saddle atop it. The horse flattened his ears as he tightened the girth, sensing his displeasure, his anger. The fact that his own wife was sticking up for the blackguard made him feel even more isolated. Outcast.

What was wrong with him?

Why couldn't he just accept the man? Why was it so hard to even *pretend?*

"You married me," Amy said softly. "I'm certainly not well-bred, I don't come from a noble family, I'm no higher-born than Captain O'Devir is. And yet you accept me."

"You think I despise him because he's Irish? Because he's not well-born?" He made a noise of despair. "What sort of snob do you take me for, Amy?"

"I know you're not a snob. You're called The Beloved One, and that's because you've always been a fair, decent man with a kind heart. I'm just not seeing a whole lot of fairness, Charles. Or kindness. And that's not like you."

He said nothing. If he did, he might regret it.

She stood there for a long moment, and he still said nothing, because shame now filled his heart as well as anger. He turned, picked up the bridle, looped an arm over Contender's poll and guided the bit into his mouth. He adjusted the noseband and did up the throatlatch, and when he was finished he turned around, his temper finally under control, to answer his wife.

But in his silence, she had quietly left him.

And Charles, standing there with only his horse, his entire family inside his childhood home laughing, celebrating and happy, felt more alone than he had in as long as he could remember—and blamed Ruaidri O'Devir for that as well.

Chapter Six

Ruaidri—sitting on the rug with the next
generation of enthralled de Montfortes gathered
around—had thought they'd all see right through his sea
monster story, but instead, he soon found himself re-
lating tales of Irish mermaids, sea nymphs, and talking
dolphins to appease their insatiable appetite for things
that only a mariner might see.

Or invent.

Above the children's heads and wide-eyed stares, he
saw the Duke of Blackheath trying to hold back a smirk
that his nieces, nephews, and even skeptical heir never
saw, and Gareth elbowing Juliet and she clapping a hand
over her mouth to still her own laughter.

Ruaidri was hard-pressed to maintain his own fa-
cade of awed, reverent seriousness, using his hands,
eyes, and voice to paint an expansive picture for the
children.

"Oh, aye, that dolphin came right out o' the water as
pretty as ye please, smiled at me and told me, 'Captain
Ruaidri, now! If it's Massachusetts ye're tryin' to find,
ye'd better follow me tail, as that compass there in yer
binnacle, 'tis dead wrong, it is.' And ye know somethin'?
Why, I gave the tiller over to my lieutenant, told him to
look out for me signals from the bow, and I stood there

watchin' that dolphin as he led me all the way to Mass-achusetts, where yer Aunt Nerissa and I decided to make our home."

The children all spoke at once, clamoring to be heard.

"What's a binnacle?"

"I want to know what a tiller is."

"What was the dolphin's name? What else did he tell you?"

"Well now," Ruaidri said, importantly, "that dolphin told me there really isn't such a thing as sea monsters, and that it was all just a figment of me imagination."

Little Mary shut her eyes, leaned her cheek down to her kitten's head, and let out a deep breath. "I am glad of that, as that sea monster story frightened me."

Augustus crossed his arms over his chest and raised his chin. "There is no such thing as sea monsters, Mary."

"No such thing as talking dolphins, either," said Gabriel, though his eyes begged for the story to be true.

"Don't you go spoiling the fun!" Charlotte admonished.

"Aye, lass, if I go telling all me stories today, I'll have none left for tomorrow." He knelt. "I've an idea, I do."

"What is it, Uncle Ruaidri?"

"See that puppy in yer aunt's arms? He needs a name. And he kept your Uncle Andrew and Aunt Celsie up all night because he's got more energy than the sun on a summer day. Why don't you all try to come up with a name for him, and take him out to play so he gets good and tired? Unless," he winked conspiratorially, "ye think ye don't have the energy yerselves to keep up with a puppy."

Excited squeals rose to the challenge. The puppy, which had fallen asleep in Celsie's arms, awoke and started barking. Mary's kitten hissed and scrabbled, trying to get away. The girl passed the struggling feline to her mother, Celsie put the puppy down, and a moment later, the children—with the puppy chasing after them and the nurses in their wake—were racing out of the room in a cloud of shrieks, screams and noise. The adults let out a collective sigh, and Ruaidri got to his feet.

Gareth approached him. "Come on, brother," he said affably. "The day's young and we'll show you around the grounds. You do ride, don't you?"

"Em, uh ... passably."

"Good. We'll find a horse for you out in the stable. Andrew? Will you join us?"

"I'm going back to bed."

"Luce? Are you certain you don't wish to go?"

"Not today. But you go on, enjoy the morning. Why don't you and Charles take Ruaidri down to the Speckled Hen and treat him to one of ol' Crawley's best puddings."

"Very well, then. Come, Ruaidri. Am I saying it correctly? Rory? Roo-ri?"

"Roo-a-ri."

"Roo-a-ri it is, then. Let's go. Best not to keep Charles waiting."

The two headed out into the freshly washed air, Gareth chattering on about the weather, asking him about America, expressing his hopes that the war would end soon, and inquiring of him what kind of horse he might prefer.

"A quiet one," Ruaidri quipped, warming to his new brother. The man was immensely likeable, endlessly affable. "I won't pretend to be the most accomplished rider in the world. I won't even pretend to be an accomplished rider a'tall."

"Oh! Well then, we can certainly walk, instead. I can show you around on foot as easily as I can from the back of a horse."

"Oh, no, 'tis fine I'll be, for sure." Privately, Ruaidri

thought of the cool, aloof Charles awaiting them in the stable, and realized he would be judged on this as well. Nerissa had told him numerous times that the family was horse-mad, and his own pride dictated that he at least try to fit in. To show that he, too, could sit a horse.

After all, he didn't need to give Charles yet more reason to dislike him.

&

CHARLES WAS WAITING for them in the stable.

Gareth, who'd been laughing at something Ruaidri had just told him about little Aidan, felt the laughter die in his throat as his brother shot him an accusatory glare. Gareth thinned his lips and gave Charles a look right back.

You're being a pillock. Give the poor bloke an opportunity, would you?

They were brothers and they were close. Charles didn't need to hear the words from Gareth's lips to understand the unspoken meaning. His mouth tightened, and he stood waiting while Gareth summoned a groom to help Ruaidri find and tack up a horse. Charles began tapping his foot in impatience. Ignoring him, Gareth attended to his own mount, Crusader, himself.

Twenty minutes later, Gareth was aboard his thoroughbred, Charles was mounted on his trusty military steed, Contender, and Ruaidri was on a bay gelding who quickly took his measure, dropped his head to the grass to steal a few bites—and refused to move.

Gareth, grinning, watched his new brother pull up the horse's head and give him a tap with the crop. The gelding stood where he was, ears pinned, head high, and muscles bunching in protest as he chewed the grass now tangling around his bit.

"'Sdeath, Ruaidri, the sun will be setting before you get that obstinate plug moving."

"He's an English horse," Ruaidri shot back, with a mixture of self-deprecating laughter and frustration. "Now, if he were Irish, mind ye, he'd be sweet and mannerly, he would."

Up ahead, Charles turned to look back, his eyes going flat with disdain.

"Do you need help?" he asked coldly.

The Irishman put his heels to the gelding's flanks and the animal jerked up his head, planted his feet, and began to back up, one step, two—

Charles, fed up, trotted Contender back to the cantankerous nag, slapped a hand across the thick hide of his rump and got the animal—still munching, green foam now dripping from his mouth—moving.

Ruaidri O'Devir smiled in gratitude. "'Tis thanking ye I be, Lord Charles," he said. "This horse doesn't like me much."

Neither do I.

Gareth saw his brother's lips move and shot him a warning glare.

A few minutes later, they were walking down the drive, the horses' hooves crunching in the gravel. They crossed the moat and headed toward the distant pastures. Ahead, Charles let Contender out into a canter, and Gareth saw him look back over his shoulder.

Are you coming?

Gareth, with Crusader beginning to jig beneath him in his own eagerness to race Contender as was their habit, deliberately kept a firm hold on the horse. He didn't want to go charging off and leave Ruaidri behind. His brother-in-law had a passable seat, though he lacked the grace and elegance in the saddle that was bred into the de Montfortes and which, Gareth thought a bit sourly as he watched his brother's form getting smaller and smaller with distance, perhaps all of them had taken for granted.

Not everyone was a perfect rider.

And he was more than certain that he and Charles combined wouldn't know half of what was in Captain Ruaidri O'Devir's little finger about sailing—let alone fighting—a warship.

He reached down to scratch Crusader's withers and glanced over at Ruaidri. "I'm sorry about Charles. He's not usually so rude."

The other man shrugged. "Ah, well. At least he's not trying to kill me, as Lucien did. And if three out of four of ye accept me, then I'll settle for it."

"He and Nerissa were particularly close. Charles is the epitome of perfection ... he holds himself to impossibly high standards. But like us all, he's made mistakes, except he's harder on himself for them than anyone. It has been quite difficult for him, the whole matter of the abduction."

"I understand," Ruaidri said, finally settling into the gelding's ambling walk. "I've a sister too. I know what it means to feel protective, I do. And what it feels like to want to kill anyone who might harm her."

They rode along in silence, Gareth enjoying the sun on his face, the smell of the wind in his nostrils, the breeze on his skin. Ahead, a pair of rabbits emerged from out of the tall grasses and sat twitching their noses before bounding away. From far off came the bleating of sheep, a dog's bark, and a farmer's call, and down in the village, the distant clanging of the smith, pounding away at something on his anvil.

Gareth glanced at Ruaidri. The other man was gazing out over the countryside, the hedgerows, and far off in the distance, the great manor house belonging to the earl of Brookhampton.

"That where that shite-stain that broke her heart lives?"

The vehement anger in the man's tone caught Gareth off guard. "She told you all about Perry, eh?"

"Sure did. If we're likely to run into him, I won't hold back on what I'm likely to say to him. Treating her like that. Breaking her heart."

"It was Lucien's fault," Gareth said. "Perry ... he used to be my closest friend. We grew up together, and it pains me more than anyone that he's ceased all contact with our family, that he can't forgive Lucien for what he did." He sobered. "Know something? I can't say I blame him, really. Perry's a shell of the person he once was. Being in that French gaol, being tortured ... he was different when he got back to England. Changed. He keeps to himself, and we almost never see him. I doubt we'll run into him."

"And does Lucien still..."

"Manipulate people?"

Ruaidri grinned and shrugged, and raising a dark brow, just looked questioningly at Gareth.

"No," Gareth said. "We're all married off now, no more matches to arrange, no more lives to interfere with. He has become quite tame, really, married to Eva and enjoying fatherhood as he does."

The Irishman laughed. "So, we're all quite safe, then."

"Yes. Yes, I daresay, we are."

❧

"Lucien, you really must do something about this situation."

The Duke of Blackheath was in the library seated at his desk, a quill in his hand and the vellum on which he was writing already covered with his bold, flourishing scroll. He did not look up, though out of the corner of his eye he could see his beautiful wife standing at his own customary place at the window, hands on her hips, sunlight haloing her upswept red, red hair as she looked out over the downs. She was as beautiful as she was the day they'd married, and he finally raised his head, drinking in the elegance of her slender neck, the whiteness of her shoulders, the way her silk gown clung to her tall, slender form.

"What situation?" he asked, though he knew perfectly well what that situation was.

"Don't pretend you don't know," she said, turning to fix her beautiful, slanting green eyes on him and Lucien laughed because as usual, Eva could almost read his mind.

"I've sworn off manipulating people," he said, innocently meeting her gaze.

"Then manipulate the situation."

He made a little noise of defeat, sighed, put the quill down in its holder and capped the ink bottle. Rising, he went to join her at the window and slid an arm around her waist, drawing her close. Following her gaze, he saw three riders far in the distance. Gareth and Ruaidri riding together, walking, their horses' tails swishing at flies. Charles a quarter mile ahead, Contender at a full gallop as he put distance between them and leaving the other two behind.

Lucien sighed again.

"This *is* getting rather ... tedious," he murmured.

"Yes, it is." She leaned her head against his shoulder. "Men have their pride. And didn't you say that the captain has quite a temper? If Charles manages to upset him enough that the two of them up in a duel, it will be a disaster."

"Ruaidri won't duel," Lucien said confidently. "Not now, not ever again, and most certainly not with the brother of his own wife. He loves Nerissa. He'll put up with this nonsense because he won't want to spoil things for her, but if she notices the tension, she'll put her foot down and take him out of this..."

"Situation?"

"Yes. And I'd hate for her to end their visit before it's hardly begun."

"If she does, Charles will resent Ruaidri all the more for it. As he sees it, the man has already stolen his sister from the family. If they cut short their visit, to Charles it'll be not once but twice he's taken Nerissa away from us all."

"Indeed."

"So, what will you do?"

"Me?"

"Well, you have to fix this."

Lucien took a deep breath, held if for a few moments, and quietly released it.

"Lucien?"

He smiled patiently. "I will think of something. Just leave it to me, my dear." He leaned down and kissed her. "Just leave it to me."

Chapter Seven

"That bloody puppy! You get back here! Give me that!"

A shriek from the kitchens and the puppy—now christened Turnip after the de Montforte children had put it to a noisy vote—shot under the great worktable where they had all gathered to beg some biscuits from the cook, their nurse, huffing and puffing to keep up, some distance behind them. Mrs. Dodman, preparing the evening meal, was happy to spoil the children rotten. She wasn't so happy when the puppy jumped up onto the long bench, put his paws on her worktable, and snatched a chicken leg she was seasoning in preparation for Lady Charles's planned birthday celebration for later in the day.

"Ohhhh!" She leaned down, reached under the table, made a swipe for the dog's tail, and came up with empty air. The puppy tucked its bottom and sprinted from the room, the prize clutched in its jaws.

"You get back here! Get back here right now!"

The children fell to laughing at her tirade, though Mary's huge brown eyes widened with concern and Laura looked ready to cry for fear the cook would murder the little dog.

Noting it, the woman shook her head and made a

shooing motion with her hands. "Right, off with you lot so old Peg here can find somethin' else to make for Lady Charles's birthday celebration tonight. You all fancy some cake after the meal?"

The children all clamored to be heard, their voices shrill with excitement.

"Yes!"

"With lots of icing!"

"Oh, please, please, Mrs. Dodman! Cake!"

"Well then, all of ye take yourselves out of here now, and let me get back to work or there'll *be* no meal nor cake for the birthday celebration tonight. Go on, now. Where's Nurse? There she is. I daresay, Betsy, if ye're getting too old and slow to keep up with these children ye'd better let it be known because they're completely out of control."

"And if you're too old and slow to guard tonight's meal from a puppy's jaws, maybe you'd better let it be known, Peg."

"Oh, go on with ye. Sit down and have a cup of tea with me. And a biscuit. Saints alive, did you see that devil her ladyship brought home? Thought I was too old to notice such things but my goodness, guess it shows that I ain't dead yet, after all."

❧

CHARLES HAD REJOINED Gareth and O'Devir after a hard gallop across the downs and, trying to at least pretend a measure of politeness he didn't feel like exhibiting, had kept Contender with his brother's horse and the half-asleep nag that his new brother-in-law rode as they walked back toward the castle. He made no attempt at small talk, leaving that to Gareth, and was glad of it when they finally approached the stables.

He dismounted and handed the reins to a groom who came forward.

"Thank you," he said, patting the horse's neck. "Give him a good measure of feed tonight. He earned it."

"Aye, m'lord."

He maintained his silence as the three of them returned to the castle, and immediately made an excuse to leave them. It wasn't entirely due to his dislike of O'Devir and unwillingness to be in his company. It was Amy's birthday, and he had something he wanted to give her.

He found her in the Gold Parlour, taking tea with Juliet, Eva, Nerissa, and Celsie. They looked up as he entered.

"How was your ride, Charles?"

"Exhilarating."

"Who won the race today, Contender or Crusader?"

"I'm afraid we did not race. Amy, my dear, would you join me upstairs?" He smiled a bit sheepishly. "I have something for you."

She put down her cup, excitement lighting her eyes. "For me?"

"Well, it *is* your birthday," he said, delighting in her childlike joy. It was one of her many attributes, and he never tired of it. "Unless, of course, you'd prefer to stay down here and enjoy Mrs. Dodman's special biscuits."

She accepted his hand as she got to her feet. "I am large enough without eating any more of Mrs. Dodman's biscuits." She rested a hand on her burgeoning belly. "They are quite addicting."

"I'll eat one for you, then. I've worked up an appetite."

He snatched one himself, bit into it, and savored the lemony confections. "Mmm, these are good."

"Go, you two," the duchess said, making a little shooing motion with her hands. "Don't keep her waiting."

He bowed, offered his arm to Amy, and headed for

the door. He was aware of the speculative whispering of the women behind him.

"Ohhh, I wonder what he's got for her!"

"Charles always gets her something sweet for her birthday."

"He's ever so thoughtful. I bet it's a—"

He shot them a glance from over his shoulder. "You'll all find out soon enough."

Leaving the women laughing, they left the room. At the foot of the great stone staircase, Charles paused. "Amy," he said, turning her to face him. "I wasn't thinking. I wanted to give you my gift in private, but these stairs are too much, I think, for someone in your advanced condition."

"Charles, I'm not advanced. The baby's not due until next month. Besides, the exercise will be good for me."

"Are you certain, my love? I can run up and bring it down."

She squeezed his arm. "I'm too excited to wait," she said with girlish excitement. "I'll be fine."

He eyed her with concern as they slowly took the stairs, his elbow steady and dependable.

"Charles, I am not an invalid," she protested, noting his worry. But she was flushed and breathing hard by the time they reached the top, and he regretted not bringing his gift to her downstairs. They could have found a quiet place for him to give it to her. It wasn't as if Blackheath Castle didn't have enough rooms for two people wanting a few moments of privacy.

But they were upstairs now, and they made their way to his old apartments where they stayed when visiting his childhood home. He helped her to a chair, and she sat waiting expectantly, hands resting over her belly as he went to the desk in the corner.

He opened the drawer. There was the box, right where he'd hidden it, tied up in tissue and a thin velvet bow. He took it out, and turning, held it behind his back as he approached her.

Her eyes gleamed with excitement as he knelt before her and presented her with the box.

"Happy birthday, my dearest love."

She clasped her hands together with a little squeal, carefully untied the ribbon, and unwrapped the small package. She looked up, her velvety brown eyes meeting his, delaying the moment, treasuring it.

"Go ahead, open it."

She looked down, tore off the tissue in which he had wrapped it, opened the box, and let out a breathy cry of delight.

"Oh, Charles!"

"Do you like it? I thought the ruby would suit your coloring."

She stared down at the ring for a long moment and when she finally looked up at him, her eyes were wet with tears. "It is just beautiful," she whispered. "I don't know what to say."

"It was my great-grandmother's. I thought you should have it."

She sucked her lower lip between her teeth and lifted the ring out of the box with reverence, staring at it and turning it over in her fingers.

"She loved rubies," Charles said, grinning. "Or so I'm told. I'm afraid I never met her."

"She must have loved diamonds, too, because the stone is surrounded by them. Oh, this is beautiful, Charles. Just beautiful..."

"Fit for a princess," he said. "Or at least, a duchess."

"I am neither."

"You are to me. Go ahead, try it on."

She slid the ring over her forefinger but couldn't get past the knuckle.

"How about your little finger?" he suggested.

She did, her face falling. "It's too big for that one."

"How about this finger?" He gently took her hand, kissed her knuckles, and slid the ring over the tip of her right ring finger. Again, the ring stopped short.

"Oh, Charles, I so wanted to wear this when we go down for tea this afternoon," she said woefully. "They'll all be curious to know what your big surprise is, but I can't get it on ... my fingers are so swollen..."

"Once the baby is born, I'm sure you'll have your choice of fingers on which to wear it, Amy. Please don't despair."

"I'm sorry, Charles."

"Sorry?" He smiled, got to his feet, and bent down to kiss her upturned nose as she looked up at him. "That baby you're carrying is more important than any-thing in the world, aside from the one you have already given us. Everyone will understand."

"I'll bring it down to show everyone, though. But I can't wait until I can wear it, Charles."

"I know, love." He reached a hand down and helped her to her feet. "Now, come and rest, Amy. I worry about you so."

"Honestly, Charles, I'm expecting a baby, not sick."

"All the more reason you should rest. I'll join you. We could use some time to ourselves, I think. Maybe we can narrow down our list of names for the baby as we wait for the big day?"

She nodded then, her sorrow over the ring's fit put aside for the moment, as he intended it to be. "I would love that," she said, happy once more.

❧

"What is that little devil into now?" Nerissa said, lifting the tablecloth in search of Turnip. "He was here just a moment ago. I'm beginning to think we should have left him back in Newburyport. He's been nothing but trouble."

"He's fine," Lucien murmured. "Been a while since we've had a puppy around here to liven things up."

"He *ate* the corner of the rug in the Gold Parlour," Nerissa lamented. "I don't think it's repairable."

Ruaidri nodded gravely. "And he chewed the leg of that parlor table."

"And he doesn't sleep at night," Andrew said, suppressing a yawn.

"He just needs training," Celsie declared. "All puppies do. Besides, he's teething. Of course he's going to chew."

"Have the cook get him a soup bone, then," Andrew said. "The furnishings will thank her."

A sudden commotion in the hall outside heralded the arrival of the older children, who were hard-pressed not to run to their seats in excitement for whatever confection that same cook would soon be sending up.

"Where are Uncle Charles and Aunt Amy?"

"I hope they come down soon, tea will be here any moment!"

"What kind of cake do you think we'll have?"

Eva leaned toward Lucien, her words drowned out by the children's excited chatter. "I'm more interested in seeing what Charles got her for her birthday."

"Yes, me too," Nerissa said.

"Aunt Nerissa ... you didn't really mean what you said about Turnip, did you?" Charlotte asked, worried. "I think I speak for all of us when I say we don't want him to go back to America ... we have become quite fond of him."

"Yes, he's our puppy now," Laura added.

"He's *my* puppy," little Augustus said archly. "And he will remain here at Blackheath."

"Why should you get him? Aunt Nerissa and Uncle Ruaidri brought him for all of us to share!" Gabriel turned to his aunt. "Is that not so, Auntie?"

"Perhaps we should have purchased the entire litter

so each of you could have a puppy," Nerissa said, sighing.

"I daresay the castle would not survive an onslaught of a second Turnip, let alone a whole litter of them," Lucien drawled.

"Litters don't usually yield turnips," Celsie quipped. "Do they, Andrew?"

The children laughed, their animosity toward the future duke forgotten as footmen came in bearing pots of tea and the much-anticipated cake.

"Oh, look!"

The cook had taken special pains to make it beautiful, and the children rushed to their seats, squealing in excitement as it was set down on the table. Icing capped it, dripping down the sides, and it was surrounded by a ring of fresh strawberries.

"And here comes the birthday girl, just in time!"

Amy blushing, took her seat with Charles's assistance. "Oh, you needn't have made a fuss over me," she said shyly. "Though what a beautiful cake!"

"Forget the cake, what did he get you?" Celsie asked bluntly, to much laughter.

Amy held up her hand. There on her little finger, the beautiful ruby and its wreath of diamonds winked and sparkled in the light from the candles. The women *ooh*ed and *aah*ed and Amy looked down, making a small fist so the ring wouldn't fall off her finger.

"I am afraid it's too big for my little finger, and too small for the rest of them," she said despairingly. "My hands have become so pudgy these past few weeks."

"That happened to me when I was carrying Laura," Celsie said. "It'll fit after the baby is born."

"The color is perfect on you."

"Here, my dear," Charles said, taking his wife's hand and unfolding her fingers. "There's no need for you to fret about trying to keep it on your finger when you should be enjoying your birthday." He slid the ring off and then placed it near her teacup. "It will fit you soon enough."

"Thank you, Charles." She smiled up at him, her heart in her eyes. "I hope your great-grandmother is smiling down from heaven in approval."

"I am certain of it," Lucien murmured, grinning.

Tea was poured into fine porcelain cups and the cake was sliced, the children keenly eying each other's plates to ensure nobody had a bigger slice than the one on their own, the adults chatting about the weather and the puppy, underneath the table, going from person to person, standing up on his back legs and placing his paws on a knee here, a thigh there, as he begged for a morsel of food.

"Off with ye, scamp," Ruaidri said, as Turnip came to him. "Show some manners, lad."

The puppy, getting impatient, jumped up onto the empty chair next to Mary and before anyone could stop him, grabbed her cake straight off her plate amidst howls of laughter from the children and sudden tears from Mary herself, who was promptly soothed by Amy and given a fresh slice.

Charles put two fingers to his brow and kneaded it, his good humor lost in the face of his daughter's tears. "That puppy is unruly and out of control."

"He just needs training and a job to do," Celsie said, picking up the terrier when he came around the table and securing him in her lap before he could get into more mischief. "He's obviously very intelligent. Did you say he's a ratter, Nerissa?"

"Yes, but I'm sure he'd be happy to learn some tricks." She looked at the children. "Perhaps you can all start by teaching him how to sit," she added.

The puppy squirmed in her lap and lunged for the unfinished slice of cake on her own plate, but Celsie had a thumb hooked beneath his collar and held him tight. "No more treats for you," she admonished. "You'll end up with a tummy ache."

"He stole a chicken leg from Cook," Charlotte added.

Eva raised her brows. "What was he doing in the kitchens?"

"It was my idea, Mama," said Augustus. "We went looking for a treat, and naturally, Turnip went with us."

"Tell me he didn't eat the chicken leg," Nerissa said.

The children just exchanged innocent wide-eyed glances, and someone giggled.

"Right," Lucien murmured, a gleam in his eye. "And who's getting him tonight?"

Gareth exchanged a look with Juliet. "I, uh ... guess it's our turn, isn't it?"

Nerissa savored the last bite of her cake, sighing in bliss as it all but melted in her mouth. "How about we take him, Ruaidri? After all, it was our idea to bring him."

"Aye, and it's not as if we're not used to him. Saint's alive, I'm startin' to think he'd make a better ship's dog than a castle puppy. That little imp has been into one thing after another since we got here. Could be he's not the right dog for a proper English family, after all. If ye like, we'd be happy to take him back—"

"*No!*"

"No, Uncle Ruaidri, he has to stay, we've already named him!"

Little Laura's eyes filled with sudden tears and one fat drop began to roll down her plump cheek.

"Now, now, everyone." Lucien made a dismissive motion with his hand and smiled at the children. "Let's not get all upset about one harmless little puppy," he said smoothly. "Your uncle is just worried that he's causing too much disruption, and that perhaps he's too much for the house. I can assure him and your aunt both, that there's never been a dog that didn't fit into a de Montforte home and this little scamp will be no different. Am I not right?"

Laura's sniffles stopped and she wiped at her eyes, nodding.

"Now, perhaps he can sleep contained in a box tonight next to someone's bed. It's not quite fair to poor Turnip if he's allowed so much freedom that he gets himself into trouble. He is, after all, far too young to govern himself." He looked with false innocence at Andrew and Celsie and shook his head. "Honestly, you two should have known better, given your vast ... experience with dogs."

Andrew rolled his eyes and picked up his teacup.

"We'll take him again tonight," Celsie said hastily. She looked at Andrew, grinning in the face of his sudden frown. "After all, we *do* need to redeem ourselves as the family dog-experts."

"That settles it, then. You two will take Turnip again tonight, Uncle Gareth and Aunt Juliet tomorrow night, and the following one I daresay it will be my and Aunt Eva's turn."

The crisis averted, the children were excused and released to their nurse waiting outside in the hall. The room suddenly felt too large, too quiet, too still in their absence. Plates were pushed aside and teacups refilled. Outside, the call of a blackbird ushered in the evening, and the golden rays of the setting sun found their way through the windows and slanted across the floor.

The silence was a bit awkward.

Nobody spoke, most lost in their thoughts. Amy stifled a yawn and shifted uncomfortably in her chair. Nerissa made a comment about going up to the nursery to check on little Aidan. Celsie scratched Turnip behind the ear, and the puppy closed his eyes, stretched, and nestled his head in the crook of her elbow. Charles sipped his tea and discreetly studied his new brother-in-law, trying—and failing—to fault him for poor table manners or anything else that would justify his unre-lenting dislike of the man. As if sensing his discerning stare, the man looked up and caught his gaze. Charles saw a gleam in his eye, and maybe even a challenge. Or fancied he did. He flushed and was about to open his mouth with a challenge of his own when Lucien, surely noting the sudden tension, spoke.

"Well then, that's it for me," he announced, setting down his cup. "Ruaidri, perhaps you might join me for my morning walk tomorrow? I warn you, though, I rise early."

"I'll be there."

Charles, irritated, decided it was well past time to remove himself from O'Devir's presence before he could say something he might regret. Or not. He pushed his chair back and rose to his feet, thinking it might be another night to take a tray in their rooms just to avoid the knave. The less contact he had with him, the better ... for all concerned.

"My dear Amy. Shall we?"

He offered his arm and helped her from her chair. She stifled a yawn, took his elbow, and they made their excuses.

The doors closed behind them.

In the dining room, the others remained around the table. Again, the blackbird called, and the sun sank lower in the sky.

"That baby will be here sooner than they think," Juliet predicted.

Celsie nodded sagely. "I'm inclined to agree with you."

The puppy awoke and began squirming. Celsie kissed the top of his head and then put him down.

"Shall we head over to the parlor?" Gareth asked. "Perhaps a game of cards? Charades?"

"Actually," Eva said, reaching out to touch Nerissa's wrist, "my musical abilities are quite lacking, and the old harpsichord in the red drawing room hasn't been played since you left. Nerissa? Would you like to reacquaint yourself with it, and treat us to some entertainment as well?"

"Oh, I would love that!" she said eagerly and, rising, took her husband's arm. Chairs were pushed back, and anticipating an evening of music, they all filed out of the room, chattering happily.

The puppy, licking up crumbs from beneath the children's chairs, was forgotten.

Chapter Eight

T rue to his word, Ruaidri rose before dawn, quietly
shaved and dressed, and leaving his wife still
asleep in the great curtained bed, slipped out of the
room. He did not want to keep Lucien waiting.

The long corridor stretched before him, portraits of
ancestors lining the walls, the staircase at the end. He
was overwhelmed by the opulence, the sheer and
brazen magnificence of it all. Hard to believe that Nerissa, who had uncomplainingly adapted to a much sim-
pler life across the sea, had grown up in such a grand
old pile of rock, where no expenses were spared when it
came to luxuries both small and large, where servants
answered every need both real and imagined, where the
family's history, interwoven through the fabric of England's itself, was proudly displayed in art, sculpture, and
even those hideous suits of armor in the Great Hall.
The place was a far cry from the tiny cottage in Connemara that his own family had called home. But Ruaidri was a self-made man, and as he passed by the
flickering sconces that lit the corridor, he speculated
that somewhere far back in the de Montforte ancestry,
there was probably some enterprising old devil much
like himself, a nobody whose ambition ended up
bringing him great fortune, accolades, the attention of

those who were in charge of doling out things like cas-
tles and titles, and eventually, this virtual kingdom.

He smiled. The resentment and scorn he'd once had
for Lucien de Montforte and all he represented were
well behind him now, and he was able to absorb the
grandeur and opulence of Blackheath Castle with de-
tachment, even faint amusement at its rather ridiculous
extravagance. But this place had fashioned Nerissa. It
had been her home, and she had left it all for him. The
very thought sobered him and made him appreciate—
and love—her all the more.

That brother of hers, though... Ruaidri wasn't quite
sure how to navigate the situation with Charles. His
strategy had been to hold his temper, stay cool, and remain polite in the hopes the man would accept, if not
like him. For the sake of both his wife and his relations
with her family, he didn't want to get into a fight with
him or take any bait thrown his way, but God almighty,
it was growing harder and harder to pretend indif-
ference.

He made his way down the wide stone staircase and
caught a whiff of food. Coffee. Where was that blasted
dining room? A footman stood some distance down the
hall, outside a set of doors. He noted Ruaidri's confusion and quietly motioned him forward.

"Are you looking for the dining room, sir?"

"Aye," Ruaidri said, relieved.

"His Grace is inside. He is expecting you."

"Don't know how a body doesn't get lost in this
place," Ruaidri murmured as the man, bewigged and liveried, opened the doors for him, a task, Ruaidri thought
wryly, he was well able to perform himself. "I need a
damned map to find my way around."

The man did not respond, probably finding such
conversation too familiar. He obviously knew his place.

*Unlike me, a lowly rogue who dared to kidnap a noble-
woman and ended up falling in love with and marrying her.*

He grinned and entered the room.

The duke sat alone at the head of the table, a news-paper and a cup of tea before him, a footman waiting dutifully in the shadows to attend to his any and every need. "Good morning, Ruaidri," he murmured, looking up. "I was hoping you'd be joining me. Some breakfast, perhaps?"

"I'm happy to wait 'til we get back."

Lucien nodded, drained the tea, and put the news-paper down. He got to his feet. "Very well then. Off we go."

No need to hire a guide to find his way around or out of this bloody place with its owner himself as his guide, Ruaidri thought wryly. He had dressed in a simple coat of dark grey broadcloth open to show a satin waistcoat of plum satin and silver buttons, his breeches linen, his boots carefully polished. The duke, he was relieved to note, had foregone the velvet and jewels he'd worn for an absurdly late dinner the night before and was also dressed for a morning walk. A footman handed him a walking stick as they left the great castle, two gundogs joined them and soon they were moving briskly across the graveled drive and out over the moat, veiled in mist in the pre-dawn twilight.

"A fine morning to be out and about," the duke re-marked affably. "My favorite time of day, really. If we're quick, we'll catch the sunrise from the top of one of the highest downs. The views there are quite spectacular, and well worth the climb."

The dogs raced ahead, and they walked in silence. The duke's stride was long and purposeful, and Ruaidri was glad of the exercise after so much lavish food. A slight breeze began to stir the grasses beneath their feet, carrying the scent of pastures, wildflowers, and earth. England might not hold his heart or offer the same rugged beauty as Connemara, but there were worse places he could be in these pre-dawn moments.

To the east, the sky was lightening, the dim glow of the coming sun coloring up now in shades of orange and pink.

"We must hurry," Lucien said, and they trekked up the grassy hill before them, their pace increasing. The dogs flushed a rabbit and gave chase, coming obediently back as the duke put his fingers to his mouth and whistled.

"They mind a damned sight better than that puppy," Ruaidri remarked.

Lucien just grinned. The strengthening light, salmon and gold, began to touch his face, the noble brow and patrician nose, and Ruaidri realized in that moment that his brother-in-law was far more at home here, high up in the downs with a new day about to dawn, than he was back in the castle. And now the duke raised the walking stick and pointed to the crown of the hill, just a hundred feet away, beginning to glow with light. "Up for a run to the top, Ruaidri?"

"If it means we'll miss it otherwise, aye."

"Race you, then!"

The two sprinted the rest of the way and reached the blunted crest of the ancient hill just in time. There they stood, trying to catch their breath after the hard run. Neither spoke. There to the east, bars of golden light shot heavenward from the horizon, piercing the hazy clouds, sending light up, up, up into the zenith. For a moment, expectant silence. Hushed waiting. A reverence for the new day. And suddenly there it was, the ruddy, vibrant crown of the rising sun just emerging, glowing orange, growing in size, now swelling and taking shape as it soared up over the vista of checkered pastures, farmland and field, the rolling grasses and dis-tant hedgerows spread out into forever before them. The land was suddenly aglow in orange and gold, and though he'd seen thousands of sunrises during his many years at sea, Ruaidri felt strangely moved.

"That was well worth getting up for," he murmured.

"And no two are ever the same." The duke leaned his head back and breathed deeply of the morning air. "It's a sight I try not to miss."

"Aye, there's somethin' magical about the birth of a new day, whether one sees it from land or sea."

Lucien nodded, and they began the long walk back down the hill, the duke marking his strides with the walking stick.

"I wish to thank you, Ruaidri," he said at length. "Massachusetts to England ... it's a long journey, fraught with danger and the risk of capture. We have missed our little sister dearly, and I speak for all of us when I express my gratitude to you for undertaking this trip to bring her home. Especially," he added meaningfully, "given the ... challenges this visit itself is presenting you."

Ruaidri shrugged. "It's only been a couple o' days. The good lord willing, things can only get better."

"Let us hope. Even so, I commend you for your restraint. It is admirable."

"Not easy, I'll admit."

"I cannot imagine that it is. But things would be far worse if you abandoned that restraint. You know it and I know it. I just wanted you to know that I recognize, and am grateful, for it."

Ruaidri nodded. "I'll do anythin' for Nerissa. The last thing I'd want to do is get into it with her brother."

"I would intervene, but I daresay that would make matters worse."

"If you intervene, 'twill injure his pride and make him feel like he's a child bein' scolded. And he'll resent me all the more for it."

"Yes, he will." Lucien smiled, his dark eyes thoughtful. "But I must admit that it is very difficult for me not to intervene. Not really in my character to just let things take their natural course, you know."

"Well then, it's a good thing we're both showing restraint, eh?"

The duke laughed. "Indeed, Ruaidri. Indeed."

"In any case, he can despise me all he likes. I've no mind to care. But it's hard on Nerissa. She loves her brother, she does, and she loves me, and she doesn't know how to smooth things."

"Time usually has a way of accomplishing that."

"Aye, it does."

They walked in companionable silence, the dogs trotting ahead. A kestrel hovered over a nearby field, swooped down on something, and rose with breakfast in its talons. Butterflies danced on the light breeze, and ahead, the long drive that led to the castle came into view.

Lucien poked at the grass with his walking stick. "So, what's next for you, once this infernal war is finally over?"

"I'll see what the Navy offers me. I'm always open to advancements, the bigger the better. I've also been eyein' some business opportunities in both Newburyport and Boston in partnership with my cousin."

"And Nerissa? Do you believe she's happy there?"

"Took her a while to settle in, but she's made friends, got herself involved in the Mariners Wives Committee—don't ask me what they do, they don't tell and I don't ask—and enjoys quite a high status given who she is."

"The wife of an American hero?"

Ruaidri laughed. "Hell no, the brother of a famous duke. Bunch of snobs, the lot of those twitterin' biddies. But she sees them for what they are, separates the real folk from the sycophants and chooses her friends wisely. Strangely enough, she's become close to my cousin's wife, Mira. Chalk and cheese they are, but they get on well."

"Ah, Mira," the duke said wryly. "A most ... memorable young woman."

"She's also grown close with me cousin, Eveleen, and has taken up watercolors. Eveleen's helpin' her hone her painting skills."

"I'm glad of it," Lucien said. "We all miss her dearly, but her happiness means more to me, and I daresay, to all of us—even Charles, though he has yet to admit it—than her proximity to us. The next visit will be ours to make, I think."

"We'd love that. The new house is built, the wallpaper and furnishings all chosen by Nerissa, and I can promise ye I'll be a damned sight more hospitable than the last time ye set foot in Newburyport."

"If I recall, it was I who made things ... impossible."

"Damned right ye did."

The duke caught the gleam in Ruaidri's eye and laughed. Ruaidri guffawed, remembering. The two of them had begun their acquaintance in animosity that had grown to wary respect and now, a friendship.

Charles be damned. Lucien and Andrew, and the fun-loving Gareth were family enough for him.

The castle was ahead, the roses nodding in the breeze as they passed through the gatehouse and over the moat, now glinting with sunlight.

"Fancy some breakfast now?" Lucien asked.

"I've worked up an appetite, I have. Stomach's growlin' like a caged lion."

They climbed the steps to the iron-banded great doors, entered the castle—and found it in an uproar.

Chapter Nine

"The ring! It's gone!"

Lucien and Ruaidri were met in the Great Hall by Charles and Gareth, a white-faced Amy behind them. Her eyes were wet with tears.

"It's all my fault," she said, her voice tremulous. "I remember putting it down on the table last night, forgot to take it up to bed with me—"

"It's *not* your fault," Charles said firmly, taking her arm. "And you're expecting. You're uncomfortable, not thinking clearly, and are tired. It was my fault for not remembering it was there."

"We searched the entire room," Gareth added. "It's gone."

Lucien was a study in poised calm. "Things don't just ... disappear," he drawled. "Surely, it's somewhere. Have you consulted the staff in attendance last night to see if it was found when the table was cleared?"

"It was the first thing we did."

"And you're certain you didn't put it in your pocket, Charles?"

"Of course I am!"

"And you checked with the housekeeper to see if it was picked up and she's holding it for you?"

"That's ridiculous, the only person who likely *picked it up* was—"

Charles's pale blue gaze, hard and accusing, shot to Ruaidri and lingered there just a moment too long before he clamped his lips down hard on the rest of his sentence.

"Charles!" Amy put a hand to her mouth. "Surely you don't mean that!"

"Mean what?" Ruaidri asked softly, his eyes narrowing.

"He knows very well what I mean, and trust me, I *do* mean it."

"*Ahem.*" Lucien cleared his throat and insinuating himself between the two men, grasped the elbow of each. He steered them toward the doors that led out of the Great Hall, keeping his body between them. "I'm sure there's a reasonable explanation for the ring's absence," he murmured. "Why don't we all go back into the dining room and have some breakfast, as well as a good look around. Perhaps it fell to the floor when the cloth was cleared and wasn't noticed."

"Doubtful," Charles said, looking hard at his sister's husband.

Ruaidri had kept his temper since he'd arrived. He'd suffered veiled abuse and insults, palpable dislike, and treatment he never would have tolerated if not for the sake of his wife. But this ... this was a step too far. An insult too fierce to ignore, an accusation he couldn't just brush off no matter how much the duke had praised his restraint. A man had his limits, his breaking point, and Charles had just pushed him over the line. He pulled free of Lucien, stopped, and turned his hot gaze on Charles, who returned his stare with corresponding iciness. "Damn ye, are ye accusing me of takin' something that didn't belong to me?"

"It would not be the first time," Charles drawled.

"And I'll thank you to watch your language around my wife."

"Charles, enough," Lucien said firmly, his eyes going hard with warning.

"No, I want to hear what he has to say." Ruaidri planted himself in front of the Army major. They were of like height and build, with neither man having to look up into the other's eyes. "Ye got something to say to me, Lord Charles? Be a man and stop with the sly innuendos and just speak yer mind!"

"Very well then, O'Devir. The ring is missing. You are the only newcomer in the house, and you have a history of thievery. *Irish Pirate* was your moniker back in Massachusetts, and what do pirates typically engage in? Theft. Therefore, the only logical assumption is that *you* were the one who took the ring."

"And why the divil would I take it?"

"Why do thieves take anything?"

"Jesus, Mary, an' Joseph, if I hadn't pledged to never fight another duel ever again in me life, I wouldn't let such words lie."

"No matter, as I only duel with gentlemen. You, on the other hand, are not a—"

Again, Lucien neatly stepped between the two men before blows could be exchanged. "That is quite enough. Charles, you are upsetting Amy all the more with this nonsense. Go, take her outside for a walk. Ruaidri, I implore you to remember our earlier conversation about restraint, and to go avail yourself of some breakfast. When the two of you have cooled your tempers, perhaps we can arrange for some apologies."

"*Apologies?*" Charles exploded. "I can't believe you'd take his side after ... after what he did, after what he is!"

"And what is it that I am?" Ruaidri challenged.

"A bloody *thief!*"

"And ye say that because I'm Irish?"

"I say it because you stole my sister right out from

under her family's noses, held her for ransom, subjected her to a dangerous sea voyage, ravaged her, and took her away forever, and I'm the only one in this damned family who sees you for what you are!"

"Watch your language," Ruaidri said softly, repeating Charles's earlier words. "There's a lady present."

Charles's hand went for a sword that wasn't there, Amy let out a little cry, and Lucien's eyes went to black ice as his hand flashed out and seized Charles's wrist, holding it there in an iron grip.

"I have had quite enough of this," he said coldly. "Go outside and cool off. And when you can treat your new brother and *my guest* with civility and respect, you are most welcome to join us for breakfast."

CHARLES HAD NOT BEEN SO angry with Lucien, so confused, upset, and overwhelmed since he had returned from America all those years ago. Then, he'd been broken, his confidence gone, and he had returned expecting a warm welcome from his family in general and Lucien in particular. Instead, he'd found himself thrown into a situation that had tested his faith in his family, and that dark time in his life suddenly flashed before his eyes all over again. Humiliation, rage, embarrassment and disgust; it was all there, and O'Devir was damned lucky the sword he'd reached for was still upstairs in his apartments.

He gave Lucien a cold stare, lifted his chin, and turning smartly on his heel, strode angrily from the room.

"Charles!"

It was Amy behind him. He heard her labored breathing as she hurried to catch up with him and paused, once out of earshot of the others.

Lucien, surely, was listening. Lucien, surely, was plotting something.

Why the hell had Lucien taken that ... that *thief*'s side over his own brother's? How could he stand there and defend the man at the expense of his own flesh and blood?

"Amy, I need time to myself," he managed tightly. "In the meantime, perhaps you might tell your maid to start packing your things and prepare to leave here immediately. It's quite obvious which side Lucien is coming down on and I won't stand for it."

Her eyes were beseeching as she took his arm. "Charles, please," she said. "I know you're upset, but if we go, we'll leave behind damage that might never be able to be repaired. You may never see your sister again."

"My sister has made her choice, as much as it nauseates and infuriates me."

"And you made your choice."

"What is that supposed to mean?"

"What is the real reason you dislike Captain O'Devir so much?"

He lowered his voice to keep the emotion from boiling up. "Isn't it obvious?"

"I'm not sure. Because I'm wondering if it's because the man abducted her, or because you don't think he's good enough for your sister." As his face flushed, then darkened, she quietly went on. "She's your only sister, and I know you all want the best for her. Nobody is ever good enough for one's little sister, especially when you're an older brother."

Charles said nothing, the muscles of his jawline hard and unyielding. He would not look at his wife.

"That's it, isn't it?" she gently persisted. "Sometimes love just has to find a way around obstacles, Charles. Yes, he did things that are hard to forgive, but it's obvious the man loves her to the ends of the Earth and back. And that she loves him. Why can't you just be happy for them both?"

"Because you're right," he bit out. "He's *not* good enough for her."

"And I'm not good enough for you," she said quietly.

His nostrils flared and he stared down at her, both shocked and angry. "That was never true."

"But it was. What was I, but a lowly colonial conceived in sin, and carrying Indian blood that, in others' eyes, made me unworthy of any status back in Newburyport, let alone here in England. And yet you, an aristocrat from a blue-blooded family, married me. You overlooked the class differences between us and made me your wife. And you did it because you loved me." She reached up to touch his cheek, her eyes pleading. "Why can't you allow the same for Nerissa?"

"Because she's my sister."

"And you should respect her choices, Charles. Everyone else in the family has, and unless you want to lose your sister forever, it's time you do as well." She let her hand drop, suddenly weary. "All of this tension is exhausting me. I really don't feel well. I'm going to go upstairs and rest."

Chapter Ten

They searched the room. Gareth got on his hands and knees and peered under the table, the chair that Amy had been sitting in. Ruaidri, his appetite gone, his nerves on edge after the confrontation with Charles, retraced Amy's steps, wondering if she'd picked the ring up without remembering it, and perhaps dropped it on her way up to bed. Lucien cast about the room, and then stood thoughtfully, thinking.

Calculating.

Eva found him that way an hour later when she came downstairs looking for him. He was alone.

"My dear husband," she said, noting his face. "I've heard all about this missing ring. Are you certain Blackheath Castle doesn't have a ghost that's up to some mischief?"

"If there are ghosts here, I've yet to meet them."

"What are you going to do to keep them from killing each other?"

"Absolutely nothing."

She raised a brow.

"Oh, I can try to hold back the tide, but those two are going to come to blows and perhaps that's exactly what needs to happen. One cannot carry that much anger around without a suitable outlet in which to release it, and one cannot accept the number of insults and offenses that our poor captain has borne without finally defending himself, even if he's been holding back for the sake of his wife and the sensibilities of his new family."

"Hmm. You do have a point."

"Ruaidri has demonstrated commendable restraint thus far, but I've seen his temper and know what he's capable of. He's a proud man, and there's most certainly a limit to his ability to weather insults."

"Charles is also a proud man."

"Indeed, and my brother is at his best when he's cool, calm, and thinking with his head, not letting his emotions get the better of him." He sighed and stared into the hearth. "What a confounded mess. I hope that damned ring turns up soon."

"Well, at least they haven't come to blows."

"Yet."

"You think it's inevitable?"

"Don't you?"

The "inevitable," unfortunately, came a few short hours later when Ruaidri, Nerissa, Gareth, and the oldest of the de Montforte cousins were all gathered around the moat. There, the captain was overseeing a fleet of paper boats, one belonging to each child. They had chosen him to be the admiral (a worthy and distant hope for his own career) and he now squatted on the grass, hands draped over his knees, another piece of vellum rolled into a makeshift spyglass as he directed a "naval war" on the sparkling water. The breeze that had ushered in the morning had long since faded, and in its absence—a blessing when one's opposing navies consisted of paper ships with no means of steering—the children used long sticks to poke their vessels into positions deemed proper by their "admiral." Gareth, grinning, leaned comfortably against a nearby tree, privately wondering, as Lucien himself was, how long it would be before things came to a head.

He didn't have long to wonder.

Little Mary, holding on to Charlotte's hand while her tabby kitten looked on, was leaning far out over the water, trying unsuccessfully to reclaim her boat with her stick. Her actions only pushed the paper craft, beginning to get quite waterlogged, farther out beyond her reach. As she was stretching far out over the water, still securely held by her cousin and keenly watched by both Ruaidri and Gareth, her father came striding up.

"Papa, I cannot reach my boat. Can you get it for me?"

"Against the rules," Gabriel declared, shaking his head. "If he helps, you get an unfair advantage."

Little Mary's huge brown eyes filled with tears.

"Aw now, lad, I think in this circumstance her da should be able to retrieve her boat, eh? We'll pretend it was a sudden gust o' wind that sent her back into action."

"Girls can't be in the Navy, anyhow!"

"They can be in this one," Laura retorted. "Is that not right, Admiral?"

"Oh, absolutely. Wouldn't be a proper Navy without you three lasses. Besides, it's—"

"Dangerous, that's what it is." Charles turned scathing eyes on his brother-in-law. "Whose idea was this, anyhow? Someone could fall in and drown."

Gareth, watching this exchange, calmly pushed himself away from the tree and grinned. "Really, Charles, I'm right here supervising, and so is Ruaidri. Do you really think either of us would allow anything to happen? They're all quite safe."

Charles stood there stiffly, hands fisted at his sides. He saw the worry in his daughter's eyes, the way she was looking uncertainly between O'Devir and himself. That would not do. Tightening his mouth, he sat on the grass, keeping a watchful eye on the children and re-senting O'Devir all the more. First he'd won over his brothers and sister. Now, he seemed to have charmed the children as well, including his daughter.

Admiral, indeed, he scoffed under his breath.

Meanwhile Mary's boat drifted farther out of reach and began to sink.

"My boat!"

"Looks like a gale might've swamped her," O'Devir said good-naturedly. "It happens to the best o' mariners. How about ye bring some paper over to yer da so he can build ye another one?"

"I am content to observe," Charles snapped.

"I'll build her one." Gareth went to the small sheaf of vellum that was held in place under a large stone and quickly began folding a piece, fashioning a boat for his niece. Charles, sitting nearby, felt his pulse beginning to pound with anger. How could Gareth entertain and amuse the knave? Couldn't he see him for what he was?

Gareth took the boat over to Mary, and the children all stood, waiting.

"Right, let's line 'em all up on the shoreline," O'Devir said. "Lie on yer bellies so ye don't' fall in, reach down, and give 'em a shove. Let's see which one stays afloat the longest. We'll declare that one the winner today, since we've got no wind to speak of."

"That's not fair because Mary's boat is the newest one," said Gabriel. "That gives her another advantage."

"I concur with my cousin," Augustus declared archly.

"Uncle Charles! Can you make me a new boat?"

"Can you make all of us new boats?"

Charles had no idea how to make a paper boat. To the best of his knowledge, neither did Gareth. O'Devir must've shown him how to do it, and Charles would be dipped in boiling oil before he either asked the rogue or even his own brother for a tutorial.

And yet here he was, stuck, his ignorance on full display to not only the children but O'Devir himself.

"This is a silly game," he muttered, getting to his feet. "The boats are paper. They will all sink."

"Charles, don't spoil it," Gareth said under his breath.

"There's nothing to spoil. What sort of idiot makes a boat out of paper?"

O'Devir's face had lost its genial good humor. He got to his feet, handed the paper spyglass to Augustus, and approached the two brothers. "Lord Charles," he said with a forced smile. "I think you and I should go to the stables. Have a talk."

"I would like nothing better."

Gareth, suddenly worried, looked nervously between them.

"Are you coming?" Charles asked.

"I, uh... I'll stay here and mind the children."

"Fine."

He headed for the stables, aware of the stares of the children on his back, aware of Gareth's concern, aware of O'Devir walking beside him. The idea that it had been O'Devir to direct even this walk to the stable, O'Devir to take control of the situation, made him see red. How dare he set the terms, how dare he set *any* terms. Charles decided to take control back. He waited until they were well out of earshot of the children and somewhat screened from them by the rosebushes, then stopped in his tracks to face the other man.

"Whatever you wish to say to me, O'Devir, say it here and say it now."

The Irishman also stopped, and he was smiling. "Right, then. I'll say it." He put his hands on his hips and the affable light went out of his eyes. "I've been doing me best to get on with ye, I have. I've held my tongue, held my temper, and held me fists, but ye're pushing me to my very limit." The last of his smile faded. "Let's have it out, right here and now. Say whatever it is ye wish to say to me and get it off yer chest."

"The ring I gifted my wife is still missing."

"So it is."

"You were sitting near us at the table last night."

"And ye think I took it, do ye?"

"Who else would have done so?"

O'Devir's face darkened. "That's an ugly accusation, Lord Charles."

"Prove to me that you didn't."

"How the divil am I supposed to prove somethin' I didn't do? 'Tis only when ye find the thing that ye'll have proof of who took it. That is, if anyone even took it at all."

Charles stared hard at him. He felt the blood thrumming through his arteries, every muscle in his body tensing and his very nostrils quivering with rage. "I wish it had been me who had chased you across the Atlantic, not Lucien. Because I damned well wouldn't have been as merciful as he was. You may have charmed the rest of my family, O'Devir, but I see right through you. You're an opportunistic rogue, and the ring aside, I can't forgive what you did to my sister."

The Irishman's lips curved in a faint little smirk, and he dug at the grass with his foot. "And what d'ye think ye'd have done, Lord Charles?"

"I'd have beaten you to within an inch of your miserable wretched life."

"Ye really think I'd have let ye do that?"

"You wouldn't have had a choice."

"I see." The Irishman slowly stripped off his coat and then his waistcoat. "Since ye don't deem me a gentleman, and since I no longer duel anyhow, I'm going to stand here and let ye take a swing at me," he said, tossing the garments to the grass. "Get it out of yer blood, get it off yer chest, let it out if only for the sake of yer poor sister who loves us both but who's sufferin' because she hates this animosity ye bear me. This tension ye're harborin', this anger ... go ahead, then. Get it all out. Take a swing at me. Give it yer best. But if ye do, know that I'm not goin' to stand here and take it, and ye may well end up with more than ye bargained for."

Charles tore off his own coat and then tossed it to the ground, his mouth tightening and his eyes going cold. Like others of the *ton* who practiced pugilism for sport and exercise, he knew how to use his fists. With all the rage in his heart, with all the craving he had to avenge his sister, to punish this man who had taken her away from them all, he went after Ruaidri O'Devir, and his fist collided with the other man's jaw so hard it sent reverberations up his wrist and should have dropped the bloody wretch in his tracks.

The Irishman didn't go down. He simply grinned, rubbed his jaw, and a moment later, Charles found himself on hands and knees, his palms in the grass, his head throbbing and blood running from his lower lip.

He looked up, stunned. Shocked. Furious.

"You bastard," he snarled, lunging to his feet. His wiped his mouth and then fisted his hands, already bringing them back up in preparation for a second assault.

"Don't do it," the other man said, taking a step back. He extended an arm, palm up as if to stay Charles. "I'm warning ye."

"Goddamn you," Charles snarled, and lunged for his brother-in-law.

In moments, the two were fighting in earnest. Through his rage Charles heard the children behind them screaming, his daughter crying, Gareth pounding up behind them and yelling for them to stop. He couldn't. Not now. He doubled down but could not get a blow in. Circled the other man, looked for an opening. And then the Irishman's fist shot out, catching him beneath the jaw, snapping his head back and sending stars through his brain. He staggered back, fell on his bottom, and saw O'Devir turn away, and through a wave of dizziness heard Amy's screams as she came rushing across the lawn as fast as she could in her advanced state.

"Stop it! Stop it!" she cried, red-faced and panting, her eyes wild. "Charles, what is wrong with you? Stop it this instant!"

The duke and duchess were behind her, strolling hand in hand, taking all the time in the world.

"Well, well," Lucien murmured, reaching down to help Charles up. "Such a sight for the children to have to witness. I daresay you've traumatized them all, especially your daughter. Honestly, could you not settle your differences a bit more ... discreetly?"

"There *is* no settling them," Charles rasped, swaying. He made another lunge for O'Devir, only to be caught by his brother's iron grip.

"Enough," Lucien said mildly, though his fingers bit into Charles's wrist with considerable force. "This is unbecoming, especially in front of the children. *And* your wife."

Charles wiped the blood from his lip. Gareth stood nearby, looking both stricken and sorrowful, Laura and Mary clinging to him. His little daughter was crying, the tears flooding her cheeks as Charlotte, white-faced, tried to comfort her. Charles felt sick. And Amy .... his wife had moved a few feet away and now leaned against a tree, her head bent. She was sobbing. Eva went to her, put an arm around her and held her close, her voice low.

"Gareth, why don't you take the children inside,"

Lucien continued. "Calm them as best as you and Juliet can. I will attend to things out here."

Gareth nodded. His voice cheerful, he hoisted Augustus up onto his shoulders and drew the children off, Charlotte walking beside him. Mary and Laura each tucked a hand into hers while a grinning Gabriel, fearful of missing any more of an anticipated fight, craned his head around to look back as they all headed for the house.

O'Devir stood alone a little distance away, stone-faced and silent. He bent down to pick up his coat and vest, and without a word to anyone, made his way back to the moat, presumably to gather up the sodden boats. *Good bloody riddance,* Charles thought, watching his retreating back. *And if you think this is over, think again.*

He shrugged free of Lucien and went to his wife.

"Amy?"

"I ... I don't feel well," she said through her tears. "I ... I—"

She cried out and the blood drained from her face as she leaned heavily against Eva.

Charles ran the last steps to her and caught her. "Amy!"

"I ... I think it's my time," she choked out, her eyes huge with fear, and Charles stared open-mouthed at her, unable to take in what she had just said.

"What do you mean? The baby's not due until next month, it can't be your time!"

"Trust me, it's her time," Eva murmured.

Amy moaned and bit her lip.

"My oh my," Lucien drawled. "All this animosity between you two has now taken its toll on your poor wife. For shame, Charles."

"You blame *me?*"

Lucien didn't answer. Instead, he nodded to Eva, who put an arm around Amy and began to help her toward the house. Charles, furious, insinuated himself under Amy's shoulder and with a backward glance at the man who had caused all this, now knee-deep in the moat as he gathered up the paper boats and oblivious to the situation that he had created, steered his wife toward the castle.

He had despised Ruaidri O'Devir before.

Now, he just plain hated him.

Chapter Eleven

"Ohhhh," Amy moaned, as Charles and Eva got her up the stairs, down the corridor, and into their apartments. Her face was white with fear, her eyes swimming in tears. "Charles, the baby isn't supposed to be this early ... I'm so scared."

"It will be all right," Charles said with an assurance he didn't feel as they guided her to the bed. "Just try to relax, sweetheart. I'm here. Everything will be fine."

"I'm frightened," she repeated, the tears still tracking down her face. "Something's wrong, I know it is. I don't feel well. Please don't leave me."

He glanced over at his sister-in-law. Her beautiful face was tight, but if she shared his concern, she was keeping it to herself. Nobody said a word as servants came running, the covers were turned back, and Amy was eased onto the bed, her gown and stays removed until she was stripped down to her chemise.

"Little Mary ... she was crying ... someone, please see to her," Amy pled.

"What is happening?" It was Nerissa, sleepy-eyed and alarmed, just coming into the room. "Amy! I was napping, are you—"

"Yes, she is," Eva murmured.

Charles felt his terror mounting. The baby was early.

Was Lucien right? *Had* the animosity between himself and O'Devir brought this on? Oh, why had he not waited until they'd reached the stable where he and O'Devir could've settled things discreetly? Now Amy was in childbirth. Amy, his sweet and loving wife, paying for his sins with an early labor and maybe their coming child would be paying too.

Charles felt sick.

Through it all he was aware of the throbbing in his lip, the way it had swollen and pushed against his lower teeth, and worried that the sight would further distress his wife, he took out his handkerchief to dab at it. It came away with a spot of blood, and disgusted, he thrust it back into his pocket. He stood there holding Amy's hand and feeling quite useless as the women bustled about, Nerissa plumping up Amy's pillows, Eva calling for hot water. Amy clutched his fingers and looked up at him with desperate, fearful eyes. A contraction hit her. She caught her breath, squeezed her eyes shut, and moaned in pain.

"Come, Charles," Lucien murmured, breaking into his shock. "Let's leave the women to this."

"I can't leave her, she needs me."

"And so does your daughter. Let the women settle and tend to Amy. You can return as she gets further along."

They went downstairs and into the Gold Parlour where Charles was both surprised and enraged to find O'Devir sitting in a chair, head bent to his hands. His thick, savage mane of curly black hair had come loose from his queue after their brief fight and through it, Charles thought the man might be praying. For what, he couldn't imagine, and immediately thrust it from his mind as the Irishman looked up.

"Is she—"

"She'll be fine," Lucien said smoothly. "My dear Ruaidri ... perhaps you can ride down to Ravenscombe and find Dr. Highworth? Bring him back with the utmost haste?"

Charles bristled. "Why are you asking him? He's not familiar with the area. He can barely ride a horse. Ask Gareth or Andrew, they know where to find the doctor."

"I am asking Ruaidri."

The Irishman was on his feet. "Yes, of course," he said. "I can go immediately."

"What are you, mad?" Charles exploded.

"Gareth is with the children trying to calm them down, Andrew is likely upstairs in bed trying to catch up on missed sleep, and Ruaidri obviously wishes to make himself useful." Lucien turned to the other man. "The doctor—" He casually pulled out his pocket watch and consulted it. "— is in the habit of taking his midday meal at Crawley's pub at the top of the hour. He particularly enjoys the kidney pie and is likely to linger until at least half one unless, of course, he is called out by someone in need of his services. If you hurry, you'll find him there."

"Crawley's pub?"

"The Speckled Hen. It's the only one in the village. You'll see it across from Green."

Ruaidri, willfully blocking out Charles's sputtering horror, nodded. He was grateful to Lucien for sending him on a mission and even more grateful to get away from Charles. This visit to Blackheath was becoming unbearable. He saw the fresh anger, this time mixed with fear, coming into Charles's eyes, and turning on his heel, slipped silently out of the room, not wanting to hear any more of the argument. Moments later, he was in the stables, where a groom met him and asked him what he might need.

"A horse," Ruaidri said. "The fastest one you have."

The groom's eyes were suddenly wary. "That would be Armageddon, m'lord."

"I'm no lord, just a captain, and I'll take him."

"But ... but Captain, he's—"

"Unless he's lame, throw a damned saddle on him and bring him out. I need to get to the village as quickly as possible."

Eyes widening, the groom tightened his mouth, nodded, and melted off into the shadows. Ruaidri began to pace. His jaw was killing him, and he wished with all his heart that the blow his brother-in-law had landed had been the end of it, the release of the other man's resentment. A cleared slate would've been a fierce fine thing. Lucien had come to him as he'd been gathering up the sodden boats, commended his restraint once more—"Unlike Charles, I know what your fists are truly capable of."— and lamented all of it with the hope that things would improve between them. Now, with his wife in labor, Ruaidri feared things would never improve.

He paced and paced some more. All the more important the fastest horse in the stable be brought out. If there was even the remotest chance of Lord Charles softening toward him, even just the smallest bit—

Jesus, Joseph, an' Mary.

Ruaidri took one look at the savage black beast being led out and felt the blood stop in his veins.

Shit.

The animal reared up, striking out with his forelegs, and was brought down by the chain that the groom, obviously fearing for his life, had threaded through the halter. Black as the pit of hell, eyes wild and ringed with white, nostrils extended in huge square tunnels that sucked in air all the way to their fire-red insides, hooves plunging and tail flung up over his back, the stallion let out a long, piercing scream, and in a motion that was part corkscrew, part buck, and part murder attempt, sent his hind legs flying out behind him to connect with a stall door with a ringing clash.

"Ehm... "

"This is Armageddon, sir. Belongs to his Grace. Nobody else rides him."

Nobody else with anything but a death wish would even want to try, Ruaidri thought, his palms beginning to sweat.

"Want me to find another mount, Captain?"

The horse reared up again, striking out with one foreleg, his head snaking toward the groom in a vicious bite.

Yes. Please. Oh, please.

"No, of course not," Ruaidri said shortly. "Tack him up and do it quick. There's no time to waste."

❧

AMY LAY in a cloak of pain, her belly, her back, even her tailbone on fire. She felt the contractions coming closer together now, and through her agony, saw Eva, Juliet, and Nerissa hovering around and above. The duchess sat on the bed beside her, holding her hand, and as pain gripped Amy and she opened her eyes, panting and breathing hard, her sister-in-law cleared a sweat-drenched hank of hair from her forehead and leaned close.

"Amy," she said firmly, and her compelling green eyes were inches from Amy's own. "Dr. Highworth will be here any moment. You need to push with the contractions. Stop fighting them."

"It *huurrrts*," Amy managed as another seized her, doubling her up and causing a flare of nausea. "I can't."

Juliet was there, taking her hand and rubbing it. "You can't hold the baby back."

"You can't hold it in, either," Nerissa said.

Celsie, looking sleep-rumpled and obviously summoned from her bed, was suddenly in the room. "Amy, we're all here. Listen to us. Stop fighting this and go with what your body is trying to do."

"But it's not ready to come out," Amy gasped, through her tears of pain. "Our doctor said the baby wouldn't be coming for another month, and—"

"It has been my experience that when it comes to matters of women and babies, doctors don't always know what they're talking about," Eva said.

"Then why bother sending for one?" Amy managed, and then gasped on another wave of pain. "Please ... just bring my husband to me ... I want Charles."

"Your husband is not likely to be the most soothing presence at the moment," Juliet said. "He's a wreck. Lucien has him downstairs."

"Then surely something's wrong, if he's a wreck..."

"He was a wreck when you had little Mary too," Juliet said sagely. "And she was born strong and healthy. As this baby will be."

Amy shut her eyes and tried to sink back into herself, seeking the cocoon of darkness and rest before the next contraction came.

"Charles," she said under her breath. "Please bring him to me."

❧

CAPTAIN RUAIDRI O'Devir had been in savage sea fights where men had been blown to bits. He'd risked his life many times over smuggling guns and food to the desperate colonists in Boston before war had finally broken out that fateful day in April of 1775. He'd faced execution, he'd nearly died when an English marksman had shot him down on the deck of his own warship, and he'd been a knife-swipe away from meeting his maker when Lucien de Montforte had caught up to him following his abduction of Nerissa. All that and more, but never had he faced the fear, the very real feeling that he would not live to see the sunset, let alone the morrow, that all but paralyzed him as he clung to the black stallion's neck as the animal thundered down Blackheath Castle's drive and then hit the road to Ravenscombe.

The long black mane lashed his cheeks, stung his eyes, whipped across his mouth with every stride. Ruaidri gave up trying to sit back and with the horse's motion; instead, he leaned over the animal's neck, watched the dirt and verge flying past its shoulder and the pounding hooves beneath him in a dizzying blur, anchored himself with both hands in the flying mane while clinging to reins that had become all but useless, and hung on with everything he had.

He had a dim idea where he wanted to go, and as the stallion's great body pounded beneath him, he hoped the creature would stick to the road and not veer off into a field. *Just get me to the village*, he thought. *If I can't stop ye, at least I can fall off, and if I survive, find this doctor...*

He didn't know how long he clung to the animal but soon enough he heard shouting through the noise of wind in his ears. Doors slamming. He raised his head and realized they were already in the village, and people were running out of cottages, alarmed.

"That's 'is Grace's horse!"

"Who's that riding 'im?"

"Whoa, there! Whoa!"

The stallion slowed, the tattoo of his hoofbeats changing and Ruaidri, never one to let an opportunity slide, took hold of the reins and pulled back, trying to get the horse to stop. "Whoa, ye bloody bugger, whoa!"

The horse fought him hard, shaking his head, and as he began to lose his seat, Ruaidri saw a burly man lunge forward and grab the reins just behind the bit. The animal reared up, Ruaidri felt himself tumbling off, and the ground came up to slam the breath from him as he hit it, the reins torn from his grasp.

He lay there, stunned.

"Someone, get Dr. Highworth!"

Ruaidri pushed himself onto his side and glared at the great beast that had brought him here at a speed unknown to nature. The hellish thing was now fretting in circles around the man who held it, head high and ears pinned back, nostrils flaring red and its tail flung over its back. Several men came up to him and helped him to his feet. He stood there bent over, his hands on his knees to still their shaking and finally catching his breath, looked up to see a man in a black coat being hustled toward him from out of a pub, a napkin in his hand as he wiped at his mouth.

"Dr. Highworth?" Ruaidri gasped, straightening to take the fellow's hand.

The man was still chewing. "At your service, sir."

"My name's O'Devir ... I come from the castle ... Lady Charles is birthin' her babe and ye're needed as quickly as ye can get there."

The doctor's horrified eyes shot to the black stallion.

"You expect me to ... to ride that thing?"

"I was hopin' ye have a proper conveyance because there's no way on God's green Earth I'm gettin' back up on that divil's back, myself. Someone here can walk him back to the castle. Now, let's go. There's no time to waste."

Chapter Twelve

❧

"Push, Amy. *Push!*"

Amy, her arms hooked around Charles's neck as she hung from him in an attempt to move things along, cried out in pain as the next contraction gripped her. Her pelvis felt as if it were being split apart, and she felt the baby's feet pressing against her stomach, forcing a flood of nausea. Sweat ran from her face. With her head bent and crying in pain, she could not see that her husband's pallor rivalled that of her bedsheets, and he looked ready to either bolt or pass out.

"Let's get her back into the bed," Juliet said as Amy uttered a particularly loud cry. "I think the baby's coming. And fast."

Eva went to the window. "Where on earth is Dr. Highworth?"

"God only knows, but we don't have time to find him or even a midwife," Celsie said, peeling Amy off her husband's neck. "We're women. I've whelped litters. We've all had babies. This is up to us—and to you, Amy."

They got her back into bed. Charles, not wanting to stay, not wanting to leave, had never felt more helpless in his life. He took his wife's hand as Celsie and Juliet urged her to push with everything she had, Eva bathed her forehead and cheeks with a cold cloth, and Nerissa, worried, rushed to the window to look out for Dr. Highworth's arrival.

Fool husband of hers probably got lost, Charles thought bitterly. *Or is halfway to London to pawn the ring he obviously stole. What the hell was Lucien thinking in sending the rotten bugger? I should just go myself, right now, before it's too late—*

"*Charles!*" his wife cried out, then screamed again as waves of pain rippled over her abdomen and stole the breath from her lungs. She squeezed her eyes shut, clenched Charles's hand so hard it nearly broke his fingers, and let out another piercing cry.

Don't faint, he said to himself. *Don't faint, don't faint—*

"I see a head," Celsie said from beyond Amy's bent knees. "Push, Amy. Push, when the next contraction hits."

Amy, panting, eyes clenched in agony, managed to find her voice. "Does the baby look all right? Fully formed?"

Celsie grinned. "I can only see his head."

"Or hers," Juliet added wryly.

Nerissa, the drape caught in one hand, let out a relieved shout. "Dr. Highworth's coming!"

"Another push, Amy! Push!"

"Come on Amy, here comes the head!"

"*Push!*"

Amy emitted another hoarse cry that ended on a guttural scream. Charles shut his eyes and silently prayed.

"The head is out!"

"Another push, Amy! Come on, you can do it!"

Another long cry from his wife, and birthing noises that Charles didn't want to think about, and then the most blessed, welcome sound of all.

The high-pitched, ear-splitting wail of a newborn.

"Congratulations," Celsie said, beaming. She wiped

the baby down with a towel and then held the squalling bundle up for all to see. "You have a baby boy."

&

IT SEEMED like only a moment later that Dr. Highworth himself, huffing and puffing from his full charge up the stairs, burst into the room with his medical case and competent, reassuring presence.

"Well, well," he said brightly, looking at the grinning women, the new father leaning against the bedpost with blood leaking from a cut and swollen lip, and the exhausted mother lying back against the sheets. "It appears my services weren't needed, after all. Is there anything you de Montforte ladies cannot do?"

The duchess grinned. "I cannot for the life of me, think of anything."

"Is the afterbirth out?"

"It is, indeed," Celsie said importantly. "We managed quite well, didn't we, ladies?"

The man laughed. "You mean to say I was summoned from a perfectly delightful meal for nothing?"

Amy, the baby on her chest and covered by a blanket, looked up at him with her huge dark eyes. "Actually..."

"My wife is concerned that the baby came too early," Lord Charles said. "As am I. Perhaps you'd be so kind as to examine him, make sure he looks as he should."

The doctor raised a brow as he eyed Charles's bloodied lip. "It is my professional opinion, my lord, that if anyone here needs medical attention, it's you," he said genially, and grinned as the father flushed with embarrassment. "But let me see your son. We'll put to bed any doubts as to his health and heartiness, shall we?"

Charles gently lifted the baby from his mother's

arms and gave him over to the doctor. He saw Amy's anxiety in her eyes. Felt it echoed in his own heart.

"This is no tiny little lad," the doctor said. "One of the bigger ones I've seen in some time. Oh, no, Lord and Lady Charles, I would say this fine fellow didn't come early at all. If anything, he's late."

Amy shut her eyes in relief and Charles, thinking of how his animosity toward Ruaidri O'Devir had kicked off the labor pains, felt a horrible stab of guilt.

"And what is this strapping young man's name, eh?" the doctor asked.

Amy looked at Charles, and Charles looked at Amy, and the two of them offered the doctor a sheepish smile.

"We were so convinced it was going to be a girl, that we didn't even consider a boy's name."

The doctor laughed, gave the baby back to his mother, and straightened. "I'll leave you to it, then," he said jovially. "And if you'll excuse me, I've got a kidney pie down at Crawley's that, if I hurry, will still be warm by the time I get back there. Good day to you all and congratulations, Lady Charles. Lord Charles."

CHARLES LEANED down to kiss his wife, and feeling the weight of every emotion known to man pressing down on his head, his shoulders, his very heart, decided to leave her in the care of the women until he could collect himself.

He slipped quietly from the room.

Out in the hall, emotion overcame him and he pulled out a handkerchief to dab at his eyes. He could not contain his thoughts. His feelings. Even his tears. Sorrow, that his loss of control had led to Amy's suffering. Anger and suspicion, that the ring was still missing. Exhaustion, from the helpless horror of watching his wife go through something so very difficult. Shock that the baby had come now when they hadn't expected him for another month. Fury that Lucien had possibly risked Amy's life by sending O'Devir to save the day in what had been a futile attempt to endear the knave to Charles. He clenched his fists and inhaled deeply, trying to sort through the noisy confusion that were his thoughts.

Had that been Lucien's intention? Had he chosen O'Devir in order to make him an unlikely hero? Charles wouldn't put it past him, and the whole thing felt reminiscent of the sly manipulations his brother had employed when Charles had returned from America a damaged and broken man. He took another deep breath and tried to get himself under control, tried to sort out what was real, what was imagined, and what was even possible.

He went to his own apartments, freshened up a bit, and hearing the excited barking of that infernal puppy, decided to go downstairs. If nothing else, he needed to quiet it so his wife could sleep.

And he needed to tell the daughter he'd left so frightened, so traumatized by his own awful behavior, that she had a little brother.

&a.

RUAIDRI sat out on the grass, watching the sun sparkling on the moat.

He picked up a stone, skipped it across the surface with a flick of his wrist and watched it sink. Stared into the water without really seeing it. Tossed another stone. Presently, he became aware of someone approaching.

"I thought I might find you here," his wife said, sitting beside him.

"And why's that, *mo grá?*"

"Because it's water. You are a mariner. You're drawn to it like a bee to a flower."

He smiled, picked up another stone, and skipped it. "How is Lady Charles?"

"Amy is fine," she answered. "Safely delivered of a baby boy with a head of pale gold hair like his father."

Ruaidri nodded. Good, then. At least something about this visit was going right.

"I'm disgusted about the way Charles is treating you, Ruaidri." She reached up to touch his jaw. "It's breaking my heart."

"Ah, well," he said with a shrug, because really, there wasn't anything else *to* say.

She nestled up against him, and he drew her close. She leaned her cheek against his shoulder, and he leaned his against the top of her head. For a long moment, neither spoke.

"I wonder what's going on at this very moment back home in Newburyport," she mused, following his stare into the sparkling water.

"I was just wonderin' the same thing."

"Do you miss it, Ruaidri? Home?"

He thought of their new brick house some three thousand miles away with its commanding view of the Merrimack River, decorated with elegant but tasteful furnishings they had chosen together. He thought of the way the rising sun touched their bedposts in the morning and filled the room with the clean white piercing light that only a home near the sea could have. He had had that house built for her, on land that he himself had purchased, and it had only been possible because he, the lowly son of an Irish fisherman, had become successful enough to make it happen. No humble cottage, no row house or rented room or worker's shack, but a big, splendid, beautiful home that was the pride and joy of a duke's daughter. Oh, aye, he missed it. And he missed the shipyards and how they came alive in the morning with the sounds of axes, hammers, and saws. He missed his cousins and friends and neighbors, and he missed the salt air and he missed Newburyport itself, a place where he had finally set down roots with the woman he loved. *Home.* He yearned for it as he had never yearned for Ireland. *Home.* Away from this godawful, stuffy, and ostentatious place where he didn't belong, didn't fit in, and had caused the family nothing but pain.

"Aye, I miss it, Nerissa."

She let another long moment go by and he sensed she was trying not to cry.

"I've been thinking," she said quietly.

"About?"

"Ending our visit and going home."

He turned to look at her. "So soon?"

She nodded but didn't meet his eyes. "Yes."

"Come now, lass. We only just arrived ... ye haven't seen your family in a year and a half."

"I know. But ... it's not the same."

"Of course it's not. Everything changes," he said gently. "It's part of life. We can never go back to how things were when we were children."

"It's not that," she said, still looking out over the water.

He reached out, touched her jaw, and forced her to look at him. "What is it, love?"

Her eyes were bleak and suddenly filling with tears. "It's Charles," she said brokenly. "I cannot bear to see how he is behaving, how he blames you for everything wrong in the world, how he just can't get over or past the events that led you and I to each other. Why can't he be happy for us?" She wiped at an eye. "We should've made this journey earlier, before his animosity had so much time to set. Before it had become such a ... such a part of him." She turned and looked at him. "I was wrong to ask you to bring me here, Ruaidri. I was wrong to assume that all of my brothers would forgive you ... and not subject you to this ... this abuse."

He pulled her close. "Come now, lass, 'tisn't as if he's put a knife to me throat as Lucien did," he said, trying to make light of the moment.

"It feels as if he's put a knife to mine. The situation here is awkward, ugly and rapidly deteriorating, and I love you too much to keep you subjected to it a moment longer than I already have."

"What are ye saying, lass?"

"I'm saying I've had enough. More than enough. That when we go back inside, I will quietly begin packing. I would like you to take me home."

Chapter Thirteen

❧

"What? They're leaving?" The duchess of Blackheath drew herself up and beheld the maid standing before her. "Oh, no, that will not do."

"It's true, your Grace. I was in tidying up Lady Charles's bed and she told me herself. Said she despairs of her husband ever warming up to the captain and she feels sad about ruining things. She wants to go home to Lynmouth Park so the family can enjoy Lady Nerissa's visit without complications caused by her and Lord Charles's presence."

"That's ridiculous," Eva snapped. "She just had a baby. He doesn't even have a name yet! She needs to rest."

"I told her that, your Grace. But she's determined."

"This nonsense needs to stop, right now."

Eva strode out of the room, down the hall, and out-side. The sun was shining, and a warm breeze moved through the copper beeches, dappling the grass. The air was sweet with the smell of roses, and it pained her to think that the day could look so perfect on the outside, when in reality, there was a growing crisis on their hands.

She found Lucien in the stables.

He looked up when he saw her, his smile warming.

"My dear Eva," he said. "Did you know that of all the horses in this stable, it was Armageddon that fool brother-in-law of ours chose to bring Dr. Highworth back to us?"

"And he lived to tell about it?"

"It defies the imagination, really. Especially as he's a mariner, not a natural horseman. I must confess I thought highly of his courage before, but this raises things to a whole new level."

"Lucien, I have something to tell you."

"What, that Charles and Amy are planning to leave us? As well as the captain and my dear little sister?"

"No!"

"Yes, I'm afraid."

"How do you know all this?"

He grinned. "How do I know anything?"

"We have to stop this."

"Have no fear, my dear. I will think of something."

"Well, you'd better think of it quickly, as we're running out of time."

They emerged out into the sunlight, and from inside the house came the sounds of shrieking.

"Git back here, ye mangy rascal! Give me that!"

They paused, watching the puppy come streaking toward them with what looked like a joint of lamb in its mouth. In full flight behind him was the cook, waving her arms, her face flushed and red. The race was no contest. The puppy broke into a run, easily darted out of the woman's reach, and shot past them, where it found refuge behind the gatehouse with its prize.

"Your Graces!" the woman said, aghast at running into her employers. She dropped into a curtsey.

"It is quite all right, Mrs. Dodman," Lucien murmured. "I daresay the little fellow worked hard for his prize."

"That was going to be tonight's meal, your Grace," she lamented. "I am so sorry, how he got down into the kitchens is beyond my guess, and he climbed right up on the stool and leaped onto the table and took it right from beneath my nose!"

"Yes, he does need ... training," Lucien concurred. "In all honestly, Mrs. Dodman, I do not fancy lamb tonight, anyhow. Do you, Eva?"

"No, I have a craving for poultry, actually."

"So be it, then," Lucien said smoothly. "Chicken will do. Crisis averted."

The woman curtsied, and picking up her skirts, hustled back to the house. A moment later, Charlotte, Gabriel, and Mary appeared, obviously searching for something. The tabby kitten was in Mary's arms.

"Hello, children. Where is Nurse?" Eva inquired.

They exchanged glances. "She is with the little ones," Charlotte explained, her eyes uncertain. "We don't need her constant supervision, so we decided to—"

"Do something else," Gabriel interjected.

Lucien looked at them thoughtfully and tapped a finger, once, against his lips. "And what might it be that you're looking for?"

Mary's eyes got huge, and Charlotte and Gabriel exchanged looks of false surprise. "Looking for? Why, we're just out ... out having a stroll!" Gabriel said quickly.

"Now, now," Lucien said, kneeling to their level. "You children do know that I am aware of pretty much everything that goes on around this old castle, do you not?"

Now Charlotte's and Gabriel's eyes got as wide as Mary's. Gabriel's throat moved.

Their uncle reached out a hand and smoothed Mary's hair. He adopted a conspiratorial smile. "I've a feeling you three have been plaguing Mrs. Dodman by sneaking that puppy down into her kitchens. Is that not so?"

Gabriel's mouth dropped open and he looked quickly at his sister. The admission of guilt was written all over him.

"Don't blame Mary or Charlotte," he said bravely. "It was my idea."

"Your father was quite the prankster when he was a boy," Lucien said. "I see that you take after him in more ways than one."

The boy hung his head, but not before Lucien saw the telltale sparkle of mischief in his eyes. "Yes, Uncle Lucien."

"You've also upset poor Mrs. Dodman," Lucien continued. "I think you owe her an apology."

The boy nodded, stared down at his feet, and shot his sister a look of barely controlled laughter.

"Furthermore," Lucien said, "a young puppy shouldn't be eating a roast of meat, especially something full of fat. It will upset his stomach. You wouldn't want that for little Turnip now, would you?"

Mary looked up then, her eyes wide. She clutched the kitten to herself. "We didn't think of that..."

"You didn't think of it because you were following along with Gabriel's mischief," Lucien said.

Gabriel raised his head and met his uncle's black eyes, trying to determine if he was in trouble or not, and if so, just how much. "Are you going to tell Papa?"

"I don't know yet." Lucien made a pretense of looking at Eva for consultation. "Should I tell him about this ... incident, my dear?"

She folded her arms and pretended to be deep in thought. "I think we should retire to the library and discuss it."

"A fine idea," Lucien said. He stood up, ruffling the boy's hair and knowing that while an apology to the beleaguered cook might be forthcoming, contrition wasn't going to follow it. "Now run along back to Nurse," he said. "She must be worried."

The children bolted.

.

❧

Ruaidri escorted his wife up the stairs so she could start getting her things together. She had learned to make do without a maid during their time together, and packing her own belongings was something she took for granted now. It was a far cry from the way she'd lived when she had last resided in this castle.

He then went looking for the duke.

"Ah, Ruaidri," Lucien said, looking up from his desk after Ruaidri had knocked on the library door. "I have been expecting you. Come in."

"Expecting me?"

The duke just smiled and moved toward a small cabinet.

Ruaidri shut the door behind him. He took a chair and sat, and a moment later, Lucien had found a bottle of brandy and was pouring them both a drink.

"I came to deliver some bad news," Ruaidri said. "It pains me to say this, given that we just got here, but—"

"I will spare you the sorrow of delivering it. I already know."

Ruaidri just looked at him.

"While it behooves and amuses me to let everyone think I'm quite omniscient, the truth in this instance is no mystery." Lucien took a seat and sipped his drink. "The news was brought to me by my valet, who heard it from one of the maids. Most unfortunate, especially as Charles and Amy are also planning to depart. Not quite the reunion I had hoped for, or envisioned, I must confess."

Ruaidri let out his breath. "Nerissa ... she's the one who wants to go. I've a tough skin, I can put up with it, but she cares about me, and it pains her."

"It pains all of us. Including, I daresay, Charles."

Ruaidri took a sip of brandy and raised his brows. "Charles?"

"My brother is a good man but a conflicted one, and he holds standards of perfection that are unimaginable to most people. Having come this far in his display of animosity toward you, there is no way out for him at this point without squandering his pride. He also feels that as a brother, he's failed Nerissa since he was not the one to go looking for her during that ... unfortunate business a year and a half ago. He blames himself, I think, and it only adds to his torment."

"There are four of ye. Four brothers, for one sister. Andrew offered himself up in trade for her and you came after them both. Ye're the head of the family, not Charles. What does he expect?"

"As I say, his personal standards are impossibly high."

Ruaidri took another sip of the brandy. "I don't know what I can do to improve things between us. Saints alive, I've tried."

"I know you have."

Ruaidri swirled the brandy in his glass.

"I know you invited him to purge his anger by opening yourself up to his fists," Lucien continued. "I know that you've held your tongue in the face of numerous insults. And—" Lucien smiled —"I also know that you risked your very life by taking Armageddon to get Dr. Highworth because he was the fastest horse in the stable."

"'Twas nothing," Ruaidri said, shrugging, though he felt his knees go soft at the memory of that hellish ride into town aboard the equine Satan.

"You saved the day and might possibly have saved Charles's wife had things gone badly, and you did so at great risk to yourself. You have done more than anyone could ask for or expect in an attempt to win my brother's friendship, or if not, at least his acceptance. I had hoped your ride aboard my little ... pet ... would soften him, but I fear it's had the opposite effect. He now feels beholden to you as well as stuck in his inability to forgive either you, or himself."

"I don't think he's ever goin' to forgive."

"And if you both leave here without resolving this nonsense, his relationship with his sister will be permanently ruined. There will be lasting resentments all around. Oh, no, Ruaidri. That will not do."

"What would you have me do?"

Lucien let out a heavy sigh. "I had thought that seeing how happy his sister is with you would have been enough. I had thought that saving his wife might've been enough."

"His wife did just fine without the doctor," Ruaidri said, without lament.

The duke got up, and carrying his glass, moved to the window. He stood there for a long moment, quietly perusing the downs that fell away to the village of Ravenscombe in the valley below. Ruaidri could not know that many a hapless person had borne the consequences of Blackheath's thoughts as he'd stood there many a time before in that very same spot, gazing out over those very same hills.

And scheming.

As indeed, Lucien was. He sipped his brandy and stood there for a long time, the glass dangling from his fingers. On the lawn below, he saw the children playing on the grass under the copper beeches, their nurse sitting on a blanket and reading them a story, the kitten asleep in Mary's arms. And there, off near the gatehouse was the puppy, both paws over the bone that was all that remained of the lamb leg that was to have been tonight's meal. Lucien gazed for a long, long time at the terrier as he gnawed away at his prize, and Ruaidri did not see the little smile that came over that dark and aristocratic face.

I had thought that saving your wife might've done it, Charles, Lucien thought.

But there were some things a man valued even more than his wife.

He turned around and smiled at his brother-in-law. "A picnic," he said thoughtfully. "Late this afternoon, in place of tea. With all of us together for what might be the last time."

Chapter Fourteen

There was cold chicken, fresh lettuce salad, rolls with butter and strawberry jam, and lemonade for the children. Little sugared cakes, and pots of tea for the adults.

And there was also tension.

Too much of it.

Gareth felt it as he and Juliet made their way out onto the lawn later that afternoon and shaking out a blanket onto the grass, sat with their plates of food.

"I can't believe they're leaving," Juliet said sadly. "How ridiculous. This was supposed to be a loving family reunion and instead it's been one awful thing after another."

"I know," Gareth said, watching as Turnip, finally finished with his prize, went trotting to the blanket on which Andrew and Celsie, Nerissa and her captain all sat together, laughing. Ruaidri O'Devir bounced his young son on his knee, and he seemed in fine spirits despite all that had occurred. *The man must have the patience of a saint*, Gareth thought with no small degree of admiration. He would have lost his temper by now.

Long before now.

He raised his gaze and looked to his right. There, some distance away, Charles sat on a blanket, alone, except for his daughter. His proud back was toward the others, his face like a stone. Mary leaned against his knee, a plate on her lap, and every so often the child looked back toward the castle where her mother, exhausted from childbirth, still lay abed with her new little brother.

"Papa," she said, her voice carrying on the evening breeze to Gareth and Juliet, "I wish Mama could come out and sit with us. We're all by ourselves over here. May I go play with my cousins?"

Gareth saw his brother look down at his daughter. "And leave me all alone?" he said teasingly, but there was a note of sorrow in his words.

The child nodded, but her huge dark eyes were envious as she watched her cousins some distance away. Augustus, on a small pony that was led by Charlotte, declaring quite loftily that he did not need for her to hold the reins as he was quite able to ride all by himself. Andrew and Celsie's daughter, Laura, tagging along beside them, asking when it would be her turn for a ride. Gabriel, calling the puppy to him and sneaking him a piece of chicken.

"Gabriel, that is enough food for him!" Juliet admonished. "You're going to make him sick."

"But, Mama, he likes it!"

Juliet shook her head and exchanged a glance with her husband. "He's too much like you."

Gareth only laughed, and his gaze again went to his brother, now lifting little Mary to her feet and permitting her to go join her cousins. The child ran off, leaving Charles alone.

"We should go sit with him," Gareth said.

Juliet nodded, picked up her plate and teacup, and walked with her husband over to where Charles sat on his blanket.

"Want some company?"

Charles looked up and smiled with what looked almost like relief. "I would indeed."

Gareth and Juliet lowered themselves to the blanket. A footman approached, refreshed Juliet's tea, and moved off to where the others, their laughter carrying on the breeze, sat.

"What's this about you and Amy leaving tomorrow?" Gareth said, at length.

"It is necessary."

"Why?"

"What do you mean, why? Isn't it obvious?"

Gareth shrugged. "What's obvious is that Amy just had a baby and needs to rest."

"Then she can stay here, and I'll return home alone."

Juliet reached out and touched his wrist. "You should stay, Charles. Nothing broken ever gets fixed by giving up."

Charles shot a glance over his shoulder at the Irishman, who was guffawing at something Andrew had said. "What is there to fix? I despise him and he despises me. It's as simple as that."

"Can't you just pretend some civility for the sake of our sister?" Gareth asked.

"You know me well enough to know I can't pretend anything."

Gareth breathed a heavy sigh and watched as Turnip bounced into Celsie's lap. She had just been lifting a small cake to her mouth and gave a little shriek as the puppy snatched it from her fingers and shot away with his prize. Gareth couldn't help laughing. She cupped a hand to her mouth and called out, "You and Juliet can have this rogue tonight, after all! You won't be laughing, then!"

"Nerissa and I'll take him," Ruaidri O'Devir said. "'Tis only fair, since we thrust him on you all."

"Hope he keeps you awake the entire bloody night,"

Charles muttered, but the comment was heard by the others, and the Irishman himself. His face went still, he put his plate down on the blanket, wiped his mouth with a napkin, and stood.

"Did you have to go and say that?" Gareth snapped, tensing up as Ruaidri, with Nerissa watching anxiously behind him, approached.

"Ye know, Lord Charles," the Irishman said, "one of many things a mariner develops is good eyesight. And good hearin'. Nerissa and I'll be on our way home tomorrow and I hope you and yer sister can at least have something of a visit before we go."

"What do you mean, you're leaving?"

"Just as I said."

"You just bloody got here," Charles snapped.

"Aye, well, 'tisn't as if the welcome's been a warm one, and yer sister, now, she's feelin' it. She asked me to take her home and while I'd like to stay and see her visit her family she's been missin' so much, I'm also pledged to make her happy, and make her happy I will. If she wants to leave tomorrow, we'll leave."

"Oh, lovely," Charles said acidly. "And how is that supposed to make me feel?"

"'Tis yer choice on how it makes ye feel. If me wife wants to go home, I'm takin' her home."

"This *is* her home."

"This *was* her home. It's not any longer. She's unhappy."

Charles got to his feet. "You're right this *was* her home, until *you* came along."

Gareth stood up as well. "Charles, let's go inside. Now."

"No, Gareth, back off. He and I have something to finish before he leaves, and it's time we see to it."

The captain just looked at him, his eyes shadowed by sorrow. "I don't want to fight ye, Lord Charles."

"Let's go to the stables and finish what we started, right now."

"No."

"What do you mean, no? Are you a coward, as well as a knave?"

"I won't lay a hand on the man me wife loves. Her own brother."

Charles reached out and shoved him hard, and with a curse, Andrew leapt to his feet and came running. "Stop it," he snarled. "This is ridiculous."

"This isn't going to end until I see him pay for what he did to Nerissa."

Nerissa herself was suddenly there, her eyes furious, a napkin still in her hand. "Charles, I don't know how to make this any clearer to you than I've already done but hear me and hear me well. I love my husband, he loves me, and I am happy. *Happy!* Why isn't that enough for you?"

"Because I see things the rest of you don't!"

"Like what?"

"That ring hasn't turned up, has it?"

The Irishman's face went dark and angry. "That's one too many times ye've accused me of somethin' I didn't do. Ye're welcome to search our apartments, our trunks, me very pockets if ye like. Go ahead. Turn the place upside down if that's what ye want. I've nothin' to hide. And when ye don't find it, and ye won't, I'll be expectin' an apology."

Charles lunged again for Ruaidri and was caught by both Gareth and Andrew before he could reach him. He stood there glaring at him, quivering with rage.

"That will be the damned day," he said hotly. "If you think—"

"Well, well," drawled an urbane voice, and everyone turned. There was Lucien strolling toward them from across the lawn with Eva beside him. In his arms, Mary's kitten struggled to get loose.

"Lucien!"

"I can't return to the house for five minutes to get a shawl for the duchess and you ... *children* start misbehaving," he murmured. "Such a terrible example you set for the real youngsters."

Ruaidri looked down, toeing the grass, and at that moment, Charles ripped loose and went for him.

It all happened at once. Charles collided with Ruaidri, Ruaidri went down under the attack, and a moment later, Charles was pummeling the Irishman.

"Charles! Charles, stop it!" screamed Nerissa.

Andrew and Gareth tried to grab their brother and haul him off Ruaidri, but the two were rolling around on the grass and fists were flying. Turnip, seeing what looked like a game, came running, yapping at the top of his lungs as he tried to dive between the two men. The children started wailing, the pony spooked, dumping the lordly young Augustus on his bottom before bolting off toward the stable, and the footman, his wig flying off behind him, went racing off after it.

"Lucien, *do something!*"

Lucien, with the kitten hissing and struggling in his arms, gauged the distance to the row of copper beeches, smiled, and deliberately put the feline down. Yowling, its tail puffed up like a brush, it shot off across the lawn, heading straight for the nearest tree with the puppy now hot on its heels.

"Papa!" Mary screamed. "Papa! *My kitten!*"

The kitten reached the tree just in time. With a flying leap it was airborne, on the trunk, and skittering up it with the puppy, defeated, yapping frantically on the grass below.

Chapter Fifteen

❧❀❧

"Oh, dear me," Lucien drawled, folding his arms and watching as the cat scrambled higher and higher up the tree, higher and still higher, until it was safely perched some fifty feet above the ground. "Whatever shall we do now?"

Mary's screams drowned everything out as she ran to the tree. "My kitten!" she cried. "Oh, *my kitten!*"

"Does it not have a name?" Lucien inquired innocently of his duchess.

Juliet stormed past as she ran to the child's assistance. "For God's *sake*, Lucien!"

Mary's anguished wails were enough to penetrate her father's fury. Abandoning the fight, he lunged to his feet and gazed about for his daughter, leaving Ruaidri dazed and lying on the grass. The Irishman's cheekbone was cut and turning purple, and as he rolled to his side and pushed himself up onto one hand before getting to his feet, Nerissa ran to him with a little cry.

"I'm fine, lass," he muttered, brushing himself off and turning, as did everyone else, to the tree where the kitten, a tiny shape amidst the branches, made a silhouette against the setting sun.

Meow ... meow ... meow.... the animal cried, plaintively.

"Papa, do something!" Mary sobbed, running to her father and clinging to his knee. "Please help her!"

"She'll come down," Charles assured her. "Cats always do."

"Papa, she's stuck up there! It'll be growing dark, soon!"

Meow...

Mary ran back to the tree, reached her arms up the trunk, and her sobs grew louder and louder.

"Bloody hell," Charles said under his breath. He turned and shot a glare at Lucien. "What the devil were you thinking?"

"My dear Charles. That ... miserable feline was scratching my cravat in its haste to escape. I daresay one of its claws caught my skin and I was a mere heartbeat away from getting shredded to ribbons. In fact, I—"

"You did it on purpose."

"Yes, I believe I did. I do *love* this particular cravat."

Charles made a disgusted motion, and fists clenched, stalked toward the tree. A little smile played at Lucien's mouth, and he turned to Ruaidri, who stood watching Charles trying to console his daughter. He looked pained. Distracted.

"Hmm," the duke said thoughtfully. He looked at the Irishman, assessing him for damage. "I wonder, Captain, if kitty will come down."

"Cats usually do."

Lucien rubbed his chin. The shadows were long now, the sun low in the sky and steadily sinking toward a bank of dark clouds on the western horizon. In the copper beeches, a gust of wind made the leaves shudder ominously.

"You're a sailor, Ruaidri. Do you think we'll have rain tonight?"

"I'm certain of it."

Mary was trying in vain to climb the tree. Her father picked her up and walked around the trunk, gazing up at the stranded kitten. Turnip had lost interest and returned to the blankets, and there was a shriek from a servant as she tried to save the contents of someone's forgotten plate.

"With rain coming in, that poor little thing will drown up there if it remains stranded," Gareth murmured, coming up beside them. "What should we do?"

Andrew, with Laura's hand clutched firmly in his own, shrugged as he joined them. "Cats always come down."

Some distance away, Charles had picked up his sobbing daughter and was now heading back to the group. His face was tight. Bleak.

Thunderous.

"Y'know, Ruaidri," Lucien mused, calmly watching him approach. "You could save the day by going up and retrieving the kitten for my little niece. I'm sure you've climbed high masts in stiff winds, and it would be a small matter for you. It would put Charles in your debt." He sighed heavily. "However, there *is* the matter of his pride, and if you do so, he may despise you all the more. I am not sure it is worth the risk."

"Happy to do it, should ye wish me to."

"I know you are. And between you and me, Charles is not fond of heights, so he won't be eager to go up, himself. No, no, forget I even mentioned it. If you're seen as the savior, it will make things all the more … difficult." He watched as Eva and the women gathered the children up, all of whom were staring up at the tree in horror, some beginning to cry in fear for the kitten's safety, and adopted a smile as Charles joined them, deliberately ignoring Ruaidri.

"I'm going up," Charles said, putting his sobbing daughter down and looking back at the kitten, still stuck high up in the tree.

"Nonsense. You're going inside. We're *all* going inside so that the kitten has the chance to come down in peace and quiet. Someone, grab the puppy, please. And no, Charles, please don't argue with me. Amy has most certainly heard this infernal ... *commotion* out here and is likely upset. And I'm sure our little Mary here wants for her mother. Come, all of you."

Agreement was voiced, and the children were gathered. Hoisting Mary back up into his arms, Charles turned toward the house without another word. His hand was on his daughter's back, and the child's broken sobs all but drowned out the sound of the stranded kitten.

Meow... Meow... Meow...

In pairs, the group headed toward the castle. Turnip, sniffing around in the grass, found a discarded chicken leg and went to work on it, managing to bolt half of it before Celsie, looking back, grabbed him. The servants began retrieving the blankets and baskets, the tables and food, and in the western sky, the sun sank behind a wall of rising clouds.

The wind rose. The trees began to shake.

Meow...

And high up in the copper beech, the kitten huddled, alone.

&

THEY ENTERED THE HOUSE. Little Laura clung to Celsie's skirts, and upset by Mary's wails, was now crying herself. Augustus's dignity had been sorely wounded by his fall from the pony and he was pouting and sullen. Gabriel thought the whole thing was quite hilarious. With a chastising glare at her brother, Charlotte went to her cousins and tried to console them, but her own face was tight with suppressed fear for the kitten stranded out there in the gathering darkness. Gabriel volunteered to go rescue it, Augustus, seeing the chance to reclaim his dignity, told his cousin that the kitten was in *his* tree and *he* would save it, and Charles felt a headache coming on.

Tomorrow, and escape from this hell that his ancestral home had become, could not come soon enough.

He carried his daughter, clinging to his neck and still sobbing, upstairs and then strode down the hall to his old apartments. He found Amy sitting up in bed, the infant sleeping at her breast, a blanket covering them both.

Charles set Mary down, and she ran to her mother and climbed up into the bed.

"Hush, my little love. There, there..." Amy said quietly, gathering Mary close and stroking the child's back. She looked up at Charles. "What has happened, now?"

He told her.

"Oh, Charles..."

"Lucien's up to something," he said darkly. "There was no reason for him to come out with that kitten and set it down as he did."

"You are too quick to assign ill intent to your poor brother, Charles."

"Well, why the devil would he do what he did?"

"Why does Lucien ever do what he does?"

Mary pushed herself closer to her mother, who gently stroked her hair. "Mama ... it is growing late ... my kitten. What if she stays up in the tree?"

"She won't, my little lamb." Amy tenderly dried the child's cheek with a corner of the bedsheet. "Cats always wait until it feels safe to do so, then they come down."

"But it will be dark soon!"

"And cats see very well in the dark. Don't they, Papa?"

"Yes, they do," Charles said, feeling miserable.

"Papa and Uncle Ruaidri were hitting each other again, Mama. I think that is why Uncle Lucien brought the kitten out. He knew that it would stop them from fighting."

"I'm sure Uncle Lucien didn't intend for the kitten to go up the tree."

"I'm sure he did," Charles said under his breath.

The child didn't hear and moved closer to her mother. Her tears were soaking a hole in Charles's heart.

"Would you like to sleep here with us tonight, Mary? Instead of in the nursery with your cousins? Your papa and I have several names picked out for your new baby brother here, and we'd like you to help us choose the right one."

The little girl nodded, her eyes red-rimmed, her cheeks wet with tears.

Amy drew the blanket up over her daughter and the child snuggled close, her hands folded beneath her cheek. Outside, the light began to fail and a sudden gust of wind pushed against the ancient windows. Charles got up and looked outside. Far in the distance, he could see a column of clouds, advancing with the night.

He pulled up a chair and put his head in his hands.

He didn't need to be a mariner to know that rain was on the way.

And he also knew that kitten wasn't coming down anytime soon.

Chapter Sixteen

Hours passed. Darkness descended, and with it came the rain.

It started as a soft whispering against the windows and grew steadier as the last bit of daylight faded from the sky. Outside in the fields, spring lambs *baaa*hed for their mothers, and in the stables, the blooded horses of the de Montforte brothers settled down for the night. Frogs shrilled in the moat, an owl hooted somewhere off in the distance, and high, high in an old copper beech, a kitten huddled in the crook of branch, wet, bedraggled, and meowing.

The child who cried for that kitten had long since fallen into an exhausted slumber after helping her parents, keen to distract her, to choose the name Simon for the newest member of their family. That finally decided, mother and children all asleep in the big bed with a fire crackling in the hearth, Charles had quietly kissed each of them and then left the room. He went downstairs, glided past the parlor where Nerissa was entertaining the family at the harpsichord, and walked out into the rainy darkness. He headed for the tree where the kitten had last been seen.

Please, don't still be up there. Please, have come down.

But he heard it long before he reached the beech. The meowing was plaintive, mournful, pleading, and Charles felt his heart catch.

He wanted to be angry at the innocent little animal for going up the tree, for staying up there, but that was ridiculous of course. The bedraggled creature was only a kitten. It surely didn't want to be in the tree anymore than Charles wanted to go up to retrieve it. He wanted to be angry at Lucien for creating this—this mess—but maybe Amy was right, and Lucien couldn't have predicted the cat's actions, and maybe he'd only been bringing it out to little Mary.

Like hell he was, he thought.

He wanted to be angry at Ruaidri O'Devir, but as Charles stood there in the rain, the tree branches overhead sending big, fat drops plopping down onto his eyelashes and cheeks as he contemplated this climb he was dreading, he knew that that was ridiculous too. The little voice of his conscience, which had been clamoring to be heard these past few days, now became a dull roar, and he was no longer able to tamp it down or drown it out.

I have behaved abominably.

They are leaving tomorrow. They crossed an ocean just to come and visit us all, a dangerous journey no matter how one looks at it, and I have been dreadful to my brother-in-law. I have been rude and awful, and in being so, I have upset my little sister whom I love so much. It is my fault and my fault alone, that things have turned out the way they have.

He wiped his hands over his face, disgusted with himself.

My fault.

He felt sick.

Meow...

And now the kitten's distress only added to his burden of guilt and shame. The quicker he got the poor little thing down, the better. He took a deep and bracing breath and approached the tree. This was the last damned thing he wanted to be doing out here in the rainy darkness. There wasn't even a moon to light his way. He laid his hand against the bark. It was wet. Cold. And it would be slippery. Dangerously so.

"What the—?"

A rope hung from the big limb closest to the ground. It was swinging, as though it had only recently been used. Beneath it were a pair of shoes and someone's stockings.

"Who's up there?" Charles demanded. "Gareth? Andrew?"

There was a pause. And then, an Irish voice. "Good evenin', Lord Charles."

"What the hell are *you* doing out here?"

"Same thing I suspect ye're doing. Rescuin' this damned cat."

"It'll come down."

"And ye believe that?"

"Obviously not, otherwise I wouldn't be out here."

"Well, I don't believe it either."

Charles pressed his fingers to his forehead. "It is not your responsibility to rescue my daughter's cat. It is my responsibility, and mine alone."

"Ah, well. I needed some fresh air, so figured I might as well try to fetch her."

High above the tree and its crown of branches and leaves, the clouds thinned and parted and a welcome bit of moonlight shone through. There, some fifteen or so feet up, Ruaidri O'Devir was comfortably perched on a large limb, looking quite at home.

Charles eyed the rope, the trunk of the tree, and considered the best way to begin his climb. "I'm coming up."

"Ye're welcome to, but I'm already halfway there.

Besides, if we work together 'twill go faster. Hard to see through the leaves and branches above, can't quite tell where that cat is. Maybe ye can direct me?" He stood on the limb, grasped the thick span of a branch above, hooked his arms around it, and hoisted himself a few feet farther up, swinging his legs up and over the next limb with a dexterity and ease which left Charles open-mouthed with grudging admiration.

"Uh ... yes, I can do that," Charles said, feeling both relieved—and guilty that he felt relieved.

"Besides, I've got good eyesight in the dark, I do. I'll get the kitten, bring her down to you, and you can take her back in to yer little girl, get her all dried off and warmed up."

"Why are you out here? Why are you doing this?"

O'Devir grunted as he hauled himself up to the next limb. His foot slipped briefly and with a curse, he caught himself. A shower of raindrops, shaken loose, fell atop Charles's upturned face.

"I was worried about the kitten," O'Devir said, and climbed another few feet. "Could hear the damned thing meowing from our window."

"Does Nerissa know you're out here?"

"Hell, no." And then, "Does Lady Charles know that you are?"

"I did not tell her. She would worry."

"Women. They do that. Doesn't do a soul a damned bit o' good."

"Indeed. Best to just ... just get on with things."

The Irishman crouched on his limb, stood with impeccable balance, hooked his arms around another branch, and with a grunt, hauled himself up higher, sending another shower of raindrops pelting down.

"Be careful up there," Charles said tightly, looking up. He felt his palms sweating in growing unease.

O'Devir paused, parting a branch and looking up through the wet leaves at the kitten still so far above his head. "C'mon, ye bugger," he called gently, and then switched heatedly to Irish, leaving Charles wondering what the hell he'd said.

"What does that mean?" he demanded.

"It means, get yer feckin' carcass down here right now because I've got better things t' be doin' than res- cuin' a goddamned cat who can damn well get herself down far easier than I can get myself up."

Charles couldn't help it. A snort of laughter escaped him, and far above his head he heard the Irishman laugh too.

Something lightened in his chest.

"What can I get you?" he called up.

"Nothin' right now, but when you and I get finished here, I'm up for a glass o' whiskey to warm me bones. I'm soaked through."

Charles, feeling quite useless, wiped the rain from his eyes with the back of his hand, and tilting his head back, watched anxiously. The clouds were thinning, the rain beginning to taper off. The wind sighed through the leaves above his head and there, silhouetted against the moonlit clouds, he saw the pathetic form of the kitten, huddled against the same high branch to which it had fled hours before.

"Come on ... come on, ye miserable bag o' shite," the Irishman called. "Let's go. Come on, now." He eased himself out along the limb, holding a branch to steady himself. It shook suddenly beneath his grip, and a cas- cade of water rained down onto Charles.

"Can you see her?" he called up.

"I can, now."

"Is she moving?"

"Aye, she's moving," O'Devir called back. "Farther out along the branch."

Damnation. "Let's just leave it until morning. The rain has stopped ... that cat will be fine and once it's daylight, if it's not down by then, at least we can see what we're doing."

"I can see." More movement, grunting, and O'Devir hauled himself up yet higher.

"There's no way those branches up there can support your weight," Charles warned.

"I don't plan to climb that far. In fact, I'm hopin' that as I get closer, she'll get brave and come runnin' to me. Poor mite's probably just scared to move. She just needs—"

There was a sudden crack, a rush of noise and in an instant, a shower of water, foliage, and branches as the limb broke beneath O'Devir and came crashing down. Charles was slammed to the ground and found himself lying face-down on the wet grass, leaves in his eyes, twigs in his hair, and branches scraping the back of his wet neck. Twisting out from beneath it, he clawed the debris from out of his face and staggered to his feet.

"O'Devir?" He pushed through the downed limb with its still shaking branches, searching in the darkness, suddenly desperate. "Where are you? Oh, *hell*..."

His heart stilled.

For there, a few feet away in the dim moonlight, his brother-in-law lay on the wet grass, the tree limb that had given way beneath him lying across his chest and pinning him to the ground.

"O'Devir!"

Charles ran to him and with a strength he didn't know he had, grasped the limb and hauled it from the other man's chest. O'Devir didn't move. Blood darkened his white lawn shirt, and his body was deathly still.

"Oh, dear God. Oh, my God, *oh, my God*..." Charles fell to his knees and frantically put his ear to the Irishman's chest. "Captain!"

A scratching, skittering sound from above and then a thump as the kitten, backing down the tree, hit the ground and fled off into the darkness toward the house.

Ruaidri O'Devir remained unmoving.

Horror-stricken, Charles slid his hands beneath his brother-in-law, struggled to lift him, and with the other man's inert body over his shoulder, hurried to the house.

Chapter Seventeen

"What on earth was that noise?"

At the pianoforte Nerissa paused, her fingers still on the keys. They had all heard it, even over the music: A sharp crack from outside, a crashing boom, and a thudding reverberation.

Lucien, who had been leaning against the mantle enjoying his sister's considerable talent, immediately straightened and went to the window. He parted the drapes. Let them fall shut. And then, his face grave, he hurried from the room.

"Lucien?"

As one, they all jumped up from chairs and settee and rushed after him just as the great medieval doors opened and Charles, soaked and disheveled, came rushing into the Great Hall, laboring under the weight of a man slung over his left shoulder.

Nerissa, the last in the line that had come running, screamed. "*Ruaidri!*"

"Someone call out Dr. Highworth," Charles gasped. "And hurry."

"I'll go," Gareth said, and ran headlong down the hall and out the door that Charles had just entered.

A flurry of voices. Confusion. Cries of horror and alarm and *dear God, what happened?* Nerissa absorbed it all in a shocked daze. She was aware of Eva's calming presence at her side, Celsie there at her shoulder, of Lucien and Andrew rushing forward to help Charles. Her legs went to jelly, and she leaned heavily against the duchess. And now her brothers were hurrying past with Ruaidri, who was not moving, who was pale and lifeless and still. They rushed him toward the stairs, Lucien ascending backward with his hands under his shoulders and blood already darkening his hand, Andrew and Charles supporting his legs, Ruaidri's wet, bare feet bobbing with every step. Nerissa fought a wave of darkness, and with a cry, picked up her skirts and ran after them.

The brothers moved quickly down the hall and into her old apartments.

"Let's get him into bed. Hurry."

Nerissa began to shake uncontrollably, steepling her hands and driving them against her lips on a quiet prayer as she followed them into the room. She stood frozen and leaning heavily against Eva, her heartbeat thudding in her ears, her stomach sick with sudden nausea as Celsie quickly turned down the covers and the brothers, their faces grave, gently laid Ruaidri down onto the bed. He was motionless, his fine lawn shirt torn beneath his armpit and soaked with blood. Nerissa felt a giant wave of emotion pushing up from her throat, welling into her sinuses, her eyes, and with a heartbroken sob, she ran to her husband.

"What happened?" she heard Eva murmur behind her.

But Nerissa knew. She knew because she and Ruaidri had stolen a few moments together in this very bed not an hour before, and as she had lain with her head comfortably nestled in the cup of his shoulder, he had stroked her hair and looked up in the darkness at the elegant hangings above.

"That kitten," he'd said softly. "'Tis bothering me, it

is, knowin' she's out there in the dark. Rain's coming in."

"I know."

"Later on, after everyone's gone to bed, I'll go out and see if she's still up there. I'll fetch her down if she is."

"I love you, Ruaidri."

"I love ye too, *mo grá*. And don't ye go tellin' anyone, now. I don't want to make a big show of it. I'll just go out when people are asleep and bring the poor creature down with no one the wiser. Let everyone think she came down all by herself. 'Tis better that way."

"Yes," she'd said, knowing that Ruaidri emerging as the hero of the day would only make Charles feel inferior and anger him all the more. She knew it, and Ruaidri knew it too. It was unlike Ruaidri to be willfully invisible. It just wasn't in his nature. But he was doing it for her. Hoping against hope to make things better between himself and Charles, and therefore, for her and her family so something, at least, could be salvaged from this nightmarish visit.

Voices around her called her back to the present.

"What do you mean, the branch broke?" Juliet asked, frowning. "How far up was he?"

"Far enough."

"What was he doing up in the tree?"

"I think we can all guess what he was doing up there," Lucien murmured. "Obviously retrieving the cat."

"The cat that *you* brought out and set loose," Nerissa accused.

"Easy now," Andrew said. "Even Lucien couldn't have known that all this would happen. That's unfair."

Nerissa sucked her lips between her teeth and bit down hard to stifle the great sobs welling in her throat. Someone brought a chair up to the bed for her and coaxed her to sit. She reached out and smoothed her husband's wet hair back off his forehead, seeing his closed eyes, his parted lips, and still features through the blur of gathering tears. She heard the murmur of voices and sensed movement behind her as servants filed in, quickly lighting candles and stoking up the fire. She heard a whimpering in her own throat as she tried to maintain her composure, and then her vision went glassy and the first hot tears spilled from her eyes. Eva's hand was on her shoulder. Nerissa knew she was saying something, trying to soothe her, but the words were lost on her as she took her husband's cold hand in her own, bent her head to his, and let the tears, unstoppable now, fall on his damp cheek. Behind her Lucien, his eyes dark with pain, nodded to Eva. The duchess motioned to Juliet and Celsie, and the three women quietly left the room.

Lucien took charge.

"Let's get our dear Ruaidri out of these wet clothes so he doesn't catch a chill. Easy, now. Best not to move him any more than we already have, I think."

Charles went to the door where a footman waited just outside and murmured quiet instructions for a pair of shears.

Nerissa pushed back as her brothers lifted her husband, pulled his breeches down and off and quickly drew the blanket back up over his hips. She tried not to look at the terrible, spreading splotch of blood beneath his arm and steeled herself as Lucien, taking the shears that were hurriedly brought, cut through Ruaidri's shirt.

Please be all right, Ruaidri. Please, God, let him be all right...

She took up her husband's hand once more and rubbed his knuckles, willing him to wake up, dreading that he would not. Her mind tried to go to frightening places, the what-ifs and visions of a life without this man she loved more than anything in the world stabbing at her, trying to prepare her for the worst. Savagely, she shoved the visions back and refused to think such thoughts, focusing instead on the gentle rise and fall of Ruaidri's ribs and the soft sound of his breathing.

As long as he breathes, he's alive.

The doctor is on his way ... Dr. Highworth, he will know what to do...

"Is it bad?" she whispered, not daring to look as Lucien put the shears down.

Andrew was on the other side of the bed, gently peeling the wet, bloodied shirt away from Ruaidri's torso.

"I'm no surgeon," he said. "But everything looks intact, and the blood appears to be from a deep, uh, scratch along his side."

"Probably caught the branches as he fell," Lucien added. He turned his head to look at Charles, standing silently near the door and looking stricken. "How far up the tree was he?"

"Hard to say in the darkness. Thirty feet, maybe?"

"Ruaidri's too smart to go so high that a limb wouldn't support him. I must have the gardener inspect those beeches, look for insects ... rot ... disease. This should never have happened."

Nerissa, one hand pressed to her mouth, finally dared to look. The wound was more than a scratch; in fact, she could see the gleam of an exposed bit of rib beneath a flap of loose and bloodied skin. Her head swam and she looked away, suddenly nauseous.

He will be fine ... he will be fine ... the doctor will be here soon...

She felt a hand on her shoulder and looked up to see Charles looking gravely down at Ruaidri. His face was tight with emotion, and he turned his pale blue gaze on her.

"I'm sorry, Nerissa." His throat moved. "I'm sorry ... this is my fault. All of it."

"It's nobody's fault," Lucien said firmly. He had gone

to the window and parted the drapes, holding one aside as he stared out into the night.

"It was an accident," Charles continued, his face raw with suffering. "I know that I haven't exactly taken to your husband, Nerissa, but I would never, ever—"

"Charles, I would never accuse you of causing this!" Nerissa whispered. "Please don't think that."

"I know you won't believe it, but I went out there to try to get the cat down myself. Mary was crying. Amy was upset. I was upset, too, knowing my animosity, my behavior, had driven you to want to leave tomorrow." He swallowed hard. "I found your husband's shoes and stockings on the ground, and he was already up in the tree. Did you know about this?"

"I knew he was planning on it."

"Why didn't he tell anyone? Why didn't you?"

"His intent was to try to rescue the kitten later, much later, after everyone was abed."

"Why then? Why not ask for help?"

"Because he didn't want to call any attention to himself." She looked up at her brother. "Or do anything that would make you despise him all the more."

Charles looked away and said nothing.

"He wasn't even going to tell anyone he got the cat down, if he succeeded," Nerissa added. "He didn't want the credit."

Charles just shook his head and moved away, raking a hand over his hair. His eyes were bleak. "I have judged him harshly, Nerissa. Y'know ... when he was up in that tree out there in the darkness, we started getting along just a little ... being civil to each other ... and I found myself feeling anxious for his safety. When he came down, I planned to apologize for mistreating him so ... for being less than a hospitable brother ... for my inability to move past what brought the two of you together. I had planned to make amends ... and never got the chance."

Nerissa leveled a flat stare on her brother. "Ruaidri would never have taken that ring, you know. Not in a million years. If you were going to apologize for anything, Charles, it should've been for thinking he did. Of accusing him of being a thief."

Charles looked down at the floor. At the candles glowing in the darkness, their orange flames wavering in the drafts.

"I'm sorry, Nerissa."

"No, don't apologize to me. Apologize to him when he wakes up."

If he wakes up.

Lucien, standing at the window and looking out into the night, had been silent. Now, he let the drape fall shut.

"Dr. Highworth is coming."

Nerissa, her eyes burning with unshed tears, lifted Ruaidri's hand to her cheek and pressed his knuckles against her skin, trying to stop the hot resurgence of emotion. Dr. Highworth was here. He would save Ruaidri. Everything was going to be all right. Everything had to be all right. They had a son to care for and a pretty house to return to and years and years left to enjoy. *He will be all right. Please God, let him be all right.* She closed her eyes, pressed her lips to his fingertips, heard voices outside in the hall now, growing louder as they approached. Eva and Gareth, and *oh, thank God*, Dr. Highworth.

A moment later, he was in the room, bowing to the duke and setting his medical case down.

"Thank you for coming," Nerissa heard the duchess murmur. The doctor approached the bed and Nerissa, quickly rising from her chair, stepped back so he could examine her husband. Her family gathered around her. Lucien, strong and steady, whatever thoughts and feelings he harbored, under a tight rein as she leaned against him. Eva, gently rubbing her back. Charles, a twig still clinging to his queue, his eyes tormented. Andrew standing there with arms crossed, trying to convey confidence, watching the doctor closely as he peeled up Ruaidri's eyelids, then pushed his fingers through the curling black hair to palpate all along the sides and back of his head. He tested his limbs, looking for breaks, bent down to listen to his heart, took the wrist that Nerissa had been holding and measured his pulse. Gareth hovering close, his breeches and boots splashed with mud. He'd had no time to saddle his horse and must have raced headlong into Ravenscombe, bareback.

"Well?" Lucien said tightly.

"Tree-climbing should be saved for young lads, not grown men," the doctor quipped. "You boys are too old, and I daresay, too heavy, to be engaging in such antics."

"You know what I meant, Highworth."

The doctor was palpating Ruaidri's chest, pushing lightly here, there. "Got a good bruise going here, but his chest feels intact. I understand the tree limb fell across him?"

"Yes," Charles said. "I don't know how much of its weight he took ... I pulled it off him immediately."

The doctor was now peering at the exposed rib, the torn skin. He sat in the chair that Nerissa had been in, pulled it close, and leaned over his patient, calling for a candle so he could see better. Nobody spoke as he palpated the rib, and Nerissa, feeling suddenly dizzy, looked away and leaned heavily against Lucien. "Doesn't appear to be broken," he murmured. "Going to hurt as it heals, but heal it will. Let's get him cleaned up and sewn back together. And stay out of trees, all of you."

Nerissa couldn't ask the obvious. Charles did.

"Is he going to wake up?"

"I cannot answer that, Lord Charles. I can only tell you that this wound will heal. Whatever injuries he's sustained inside, only God knows at this point." He called for a washbasin and hot water, then looked up at

Nerissa. "My lady? Perhaps you and the duchess would prefer to wait downstairs? This is really not a sight for gentle eyes."

"He is my husband. I will stay."

The doctor looked at Lucien and raised a brow.

"She's a de Montforte," he said. "She'll stay."

"No…" Ruaidri's eyes slowly opened and drifted shut once more. "She's an O'Devir, now."

"Oh, thank God, you're *awake*!" Nerissa cried on a little sob, and rushed to her husband. She leaned down and over him and cradling his head between her palms, put her cheek to his. "Oh, thank you, Lord Jesus. Thank you…" Tears of relief spilled from her eyes, rolled down her cheek, and soaked his skin. "You scared us, Ruaidri … we thought you were going to die."

His eyes opened again, and this time he managed a weak smile. "I'm an Irishman … when it's me time to die, it won't be in an English castle." He tried to sit up, but Lucien was there, his hand firmly on his shoulder and preventing it. Only then did Ruaidri note the number of people in the room, including the very same doctor he'd brought back for Amy when the child had come. "What the divil's going on here?"

"That tree limb you were on … it broke," Charles said tightly. "The whole thing fell, and you with it."

"Did it now…" He looked up at the doctor, who was motioning for a table on which to put the washbasin as it was brought near. "What's broken?"

"Nothing that I can see, but you have a significant laceration on your side. Lucky you didn't break a rib and pierce the lung. I'll clean it, sew you back together, and bind you up. It'll hurt for a while, but you'll heal."

"Always do."

A footman arrived with hot water in a pitcher. He poured it into the washbasin, and the doctor dipped a cloth into it. He wrung it out and then began cleaning the torn skin.

"Got some good Irish whiskey?" Ruaidri asked, gazing up at the canopy above.

"I'll save any libations until after I'm finished here."

"Pour it on the wound. 'Twill kill anythin' that got in there. Keep it from going bad."

"You are the patient, and I am the doctor. Whiskey is best consumed via the mouth, not wasted on lacerations and—"

"Just do it," Lucien said impatiently.

The doctor sighed and nodded. "Yes, your Grace."

"Gareth, go find some."

"I'll go," Charles put in. He had been paralyzed with fear and grief as he'd stood listening to his sister's broken sobs, the tears tracking down her face as she'd cried over her unmoving husband. Now, she was leaning down to hug him, and Charles saw him hook an arm around her neck to draw her close. He whispered something into her ear that turned her tears into sudden laughter, and he realized with a sudden, overwhelming rush of feeling, what he'd been unwilling to acknowledge all along.

They are meant to be together.

And everyone had seen it but him.

Together. She loves him in a way she never loved Perry, loves him the way we all do our wives, and she loves him with her entire heart and soul. He is her very life. Her soulmate. And he loves her too. Obviously, he does. Why else did he restrain himself in the face of my unfair, unkind treatment of him?

He took a deep breath and strode to the door.

Indeed, he has been a better husband to her than I've been a brother. Oh, how terrible I have been to him. To her. To them both. I have caused enough trouble, enough heartache, and it has cost them dearly. And he went up into that tree without telling anyone. Did it for not only the kitten, but our little girl. My little girl. I feel positively sick. Ashamed. I can't stay here and face anyone. Yes, it's best that I just quietly leave. Let them have their visit, as they deserve, in peace.

Overcome with guilt and sorrow, he slipped from the room and out into the hall. There, he found all of the wives hovering anxiously around. Even Amy, who had recovered some of her color, was there. As one, they converged on him, the puppy pawing at Celsie's knees until she picked him up.

"How is he?"

"Is he awake?"

"Is anything broken?"

"Will he be all right?"

Charles just left them and their questions to Gareth, who had emerged behind him. He had whiskey to find.

Chapter Eighteen

❧

Hours later, the house was quiet.

Dr. Highworth had long since returned to the village. Nobody went back to the parlor or felt like gathering, and weary from what had turned out to be a trying day, everyone made their excuses and retired for the night.

Turnip, having exhausted Celsie and Andrew the previous nights, now reposed in a box beside the bed in which Gareth and Juliet, woken by the puppy's sudden whining, now sat in a tired stupor, waiting for him to settle back down. They had got him outside just in time for what turned out to be an explosion out of his back end that was a testimony to—and a result of—all the food he had stolen earlier, and neither Gareth nor Juliet dared to fall back asleep for fear it was just the beginning of what promised to be a very long night.

In the rooms in which he had grown up, Andrew slept entwined with Celsie beneath the blankets, a fire dying in the hearth. After their sleepless tenure with Turnip, neither he nor his wife suffered the insomnia that plagued his brothers.

In the ducal apartments, Lucien lay staring up in the darkness as he waited for his duchess to return from the nursery where she'd gone to check on their son.

In his old rooms, Charles tossed and turned, finally got up and went to sit in a chair by the window so his restlessness wouldn't keep his wife, still exhausted from delivering what was the most perfect little boy in the entire world, awake. He dreaded the morning, when he would quietly remove himself from the house so Nerissa and her recovering husband could have a proper visit with the family without the awkwardness his presence, and the events of the past few days, would ensure. He did not look forward to the explanations, the good-byes, the protests, and surely, the silent accusations. Embarrassed and ashamed, he just wanted to go away and let them all enjoy each other's company without him.

And in a gilded room fit for a princess, an Irish mariner and his beautiful highborn wife lay in bed, his arm wrapped around her to hold her close against him, her head nestled against the uninjured side of his chest. Both stared into the darkness.

"I don't think we should head home tomorrow, *mo grá*," he said quietly, his fingers stroking her back.

"Well then, we will go as soon as you're well enough to travel. I've had enough. It's been one disaster after another, and this homecoming was nothing like what it was supposed to be. Tonight was the last straw."

"I'm well enough to travel, lass. That's not what I'm talking about."

She fought back tears as she thought of how close she'd come to losing him.

"What *are* you talking about, then?"

"If we go tomorrow, it leaves unfinished business and a world o' hurt behind. The next time we come back—"

"I don't ever want to come back."

"Come now, Sunshine, you can't mean that."

"I do mean it. Everything has changed. My brothers are all married and have their own lives, their own children, their own homes. I'm married and live far away, in a place which is nothing like this one. We're not the family we were, I don't even recognize what Charles has become, and everything is just ... different. Why should I ever want to come back? To subject you to such horrible treatment?"

"My dear Nerissa, I've a thick skin. Three out o' four of yer brothers seem to like me. Can't complain, now."

"I still wish to go home. Too much has changed and there's no fixing it."

"If we go home tomorrow, there won't *be* any fixing it. Things will stay as they are ... in fact, they're likely to get worse."

"And the puppy ... he's been nothing but trouble from the moment we arrived."

"He's been nothing but trouble since he was born. It's what makes him so charming."

"We shouldn't have brought him. I thought he'd be a nice gift for the family ... something from America to remember us by ... we're all dog lovers ... but it's all gone so very wrong."

"He's a *puppy*, lass. He's just doing what puppies do."

She felt hot tears tracking down her cheeks and hoped her husband would not notice. But, of course he noticed. His thumb came up to gently wipe them away and she felt his lips in her hair as he drew her close.

"Nerissa, love, I'll say it again, one last time. I think it's wrong to go home tomorrow, and if we do, 'twill leave a pile o' hurt feelings in our wake. It'll leave a fierce rift between you and yer brother that'll never heal. But I won't try to force ye to do something ye've no mind to do. If ye want to go home, we'll finish packing and catch the stage in Ravenscombe tomorrow. We'll head back to the coast. I'll sail us home and that will be that. But I think ye'll regret it."

She sniffled, overwhelmed. Celsie's and Andrew's

bleary-eyed exhaustion after their nights spent with the puppy. Charles's unceasing hostility. Amy going into labor from the stress of Charles and Ruaidri coming to fisticuffs. The horrible accusations of the ring's theft. The puppy chasing Mary's kitten up the tree, the little girl's screams for her stranded pet, the horrible sound of the limb giving way outside, Ruaidri lying hurt and unconscious on the bed, and perhaps worst of all, Lucien's inability or even unwillingness to *fix* this whole big, bubbling, bloody awful mess that had been set in motion by their arrival.

All of it played over and over in her mind, unceasing.

Since when had Lucien not fixed something? Anything?

It seemed he too had changed. No, nothing was the same, nothing was the same at all, and none of it, not one *bit* of it, felt right.

"Nerissa?"

"I've made up my mind, Ruaidri. I want to go home."

❧

THE RAIN HAD RETURNED, and he could hear its soft whisper outside. It beat relentlessly against the ancient glass of the tower bedroom's windows, and on any other night he might have found it soothing. Restful. Tonight though, the sound was mournful, a lament for what should have been but wasn't. A dirge. Lucien lay staring up into the gloom, waiting for Eva to return. His heart was troubled. He could not sleep, either.

He heard hid duchess's soft tread across the rug as she moved softly back into the room.

"No need to be quiet," he murmured. "I am awake."

She slid into bed beside him and up against his skin, right where he liked her. He pulled the blankets over them both, and she dropped tantalizing kisses along the base of his neck, and down his chest, her hand finding him in the darkness. She knew him well enough to know what was troubling him, knew him well enough that she would try to love away his heartbreak. His arms went around her and they came together, and when it was over, he still could not sleep.

"Lucien," she murmured. "What will you do?"

It was a long moment before he spoke.

"I can't force Charles to like him," he said. "And I fear too much damage has been done for this situation to ever resolve."

She rested her head on his chest, her ear against his heartbeat. "Charles said himself, that he felt his animosity toward Ruaidri starting to lessen. That they were actually being civil to each other while trying to rescue Mary's kitten."

"Easy to say in the face of a crisis that was almost a tragedy. Such times of fear for someone's very life tend to bring out the best in people. The regrets. But now that Ruaidri is recovered and the crisis is past, Charles will be unable to forgive himself for his feelings. His actions. I know my brother. I know how hard he is on himself, the standards he sets for himself, and he's too ashamed to just go up to Ruaidri, apologize, and try to begin anew."

"I don't understand how someone *couldn't* like Ruaidri. A person would have to be blind not to see how much he absolutely worships the ground Nerissa walks on. He's the best thing that ever happened to her."

"Indeed. It's what brought me around to accepting, and eventually liking him. Much as I hated to admit it at the time."

They lay in the darkness together, he stroking his duchess's long, unbound hair, she staring into the dying hearth, he at the bed hangings above.

"What does the poor fellow have to do for Charles

to accept him?" she asked. "He brought Nerissa across an entire ocean just so she could be with her family."

"And held his considerable temper in the face of Charles's animosity."

"And risked his life aboard that hellish stallion of yours in order to call out Dr. Highworth for Charles's wife."

"And nearly killed himself trying to rescue Charles's daughter's kitten from the tree."

"The man's a hero."

Lucien sighed. "All that, and it still isn't enough."

"And now Charles is also leaving. Taking his family, including a wife that just gave birth and a newborn baby, back home."

"A bloody disaster."

"What will you do, Lucien?"

For once in his life, Lucien didn't have a plan, and said so.

"Well, *I* may just have one," Eva said slyly.

"Do tell, my dear."

"It involves the children. But it might ... it might just work."

Chapter Nineteen

❧

Andrew awoke some time near dawn. He raised himself on one elbow, kissed his sleeping wife, and quietly got up. Shrugging into his banyan, he left Celsie abed and crept downstairs, stretching and yawning as he went. For the first time in days, he felt refreshed. Awake. Outside the windows the eastern sky was pale pink, and the rain that had been intermittent throughout the night was now nothing but a few last ribbons of cloud skating rapidly across the sky.

It promised to be a beautiful morning, the kind of English spring day that poets praised and birds sang about and paintings immortalized.

The birds were already at it. He heard a blackbird's call as it welcomed the coming sunrise, and wishing to fill his lungs with sweet, rain-washed air, Andrew headed for the Great Hall, still and empty except for its suits of armor. His steps echoed on the marble flooring. He pulled open the ancient iron-banded door and went outside.

He paused. Gareth sat there on the steps, head bent, the heels of his hands pressed to his eye sockets, his tawny hair splaying up through and around his fin-gers. On the grass some fifteen feet away, the puppy squatted, straining.

"What the hell?" Andrew asked.

"Poor thing has the trots," Gareth said, looking up. His eyes were bleary and red-rimmed from lack of sleep. "Been out here half the night."

"Really, you should've taken him somewhere else. Someone's likely to step in it."

"Ask me if I give a damn."

"Obviously, you don't."

"You're the dog expert here. How do I get him to stop shitting?"

"I'm not the expert, Celsie is. And she's sleeping. But after what he ate yesterday—"

"Indeed."

Andrew sat on the step beside his brother. The puppy finished, whined, and came up to them, pressing his muzzle against Andrew's hand and licking his fingers.

"Hard to be angry with such a cute face."

Gareth tried unsuccessfully to suppress a yawn. "Easy enough when you haven't had any sleep all night."

"I slept like a baby."

"Rub it in, would you?"

"But only because he kept Celsie and me up the previous nights."

"Lucien's and Eva's turn tonight."

Andrew shook his head. "I don't think so. Nerissa told me they're taking him back with them. That he's caused enough trouble."

"Like hell he has!"

"Just telling you what she said."

"Well, I'll take him."

"You'll have to fight me for him. I've grown attached to the little rascal."

The door opened behind them and Lucien came out. Though he was freshly shaven, his eyes were lined with fatigue, and he didn't have his usual morning energy.

"Good morning," he said amiably. "Fine day it looks to be."

"If only," Andrew muttered.

Gareth noted the absence of Lucien's walking stick as well as the dogs he usually took with him on his morning jaunts. "Change in routine for you?"

"A mere delay. I feel compelled to check that tree, inspect it for insects or rot. That limb should never have broken. It's dangerous."

Gareth looked at him quizzically. "This early in the morning? Couldn't it wait?"

"I have much to do."

"How about finding a way to keep the family from dispersing?" Andrew stared flatly at him. "You do know that Charles is leaving today, and so is Nerissa?"

"Of course I know."

"The whole damned visit has been completely bollocksed up."

Lucien affected a heavy sigh and looked toward the brightening horizon. "If you will excuse me, I must have a word with my coachman before the day gets any older. Good morning, both of you."

"Lucien, what are you going to do?"

Lucien, already partway down the steps, stopped, put an elegant forefinger to his chest, and inquired, "Me?"

"You're just going to let them all leave?"

For a moment, a shadow of a smile played with the farthest corner of the duke's mouth, come and gone so quickly one who didn't know him well would have missed it.

Gareth and Andrew, however, knew him well.

"My dear Gareth," he murmured, with a dramatic and affected sigh. "When will all of you realize I am nothing but a mere mortal?"

Inclining his head, he turned and continued toward

the stables, a tall, confident figure who had never let them down before.

When will all of you realize I am nothing but a mere mortal?

Gareth and Andrew just looked at each other.

"*Never*," they both echoed in unison.

THE DUKE CONTINUED HIS WALK, eventually pausing under the copper beech that had nearly claimed the life of his brother-in-law. A brother-in-law who was part of his family, and as such, fell under his own sphere of protection. A brother-in-law he had come to admire, respect, and yes, even to love. He stood for a long moment, his dark eyes taking in the rotted timber, the visible evidence of insects. He knelt, picked up a fragment of the broken limb, and pushed his thumb into the spongy wood. Then he rose and put it into his pocket. Whatever Charles imagined the rest of the family might think—and surely it was just that, imaginings—Lucien knew his brother was incapable of harming Ruaidri in such a terrible way no matter how much he might despise him. Still, it was nice to have proof. His curiosity satisfied, he paid a short visit to his coachman, who was surprised to see his Grace purposely seeking him out at such an early hour.

Lucien glanced back toward the castle, only the great towers beginning to glow with the morning sun while the rest of his ancestral home was still in shadow. He smiled. According to plan, Eva was probably in the nursery by now, or would be before the children were given their breakfast.

The sun rose higher, the golden rays spreading over the downs, throwing long shadows across the still-wet grass from the copper beeches, the sycamores, the chestnuts. In the stable, a groom and the coachman affixed the boot to the ducal coach and rubbed the vehicle, already and always gleaming, down in preparation for Captain O'Devir and the Lady Nerissa's use. In the great dining room, rolls, orange preserves, eggs, gammon, tea, coffee, and chocolate were set out for breakfast, an affair that everyone tried to pretend was normal when it was anything but. Conversation was limited after family members inquired about Ruaidri's health and again expressed relief that he had not been more seriously injured. Eyes were downcast. An air of sadness hung over the room. Charles didn't even come down but took a tray in his apartments with Amy, and as the sun streamed through the windows and crept up the ancient walls, it was hard to believe such a perfect and sunny day would, before its end, bring such sorrow.

"I wish you would reconsider," Juliet said. "Please, Nerissa. You only just arrived."

Celsie reached out and touched Nerissa's wrist. "None of us want you to go."

Her brothers all joined in the clamor. All of them, except the painfully absent Charles who, she was told, was also leaving this morning.

Charles, to whom she had been particularly close all the years of their childhood.

Charles, who had become like a stranger to her with his behavior.

Charles, whom she loved.

Sudden tears sparkled in her eyes and she bent her head to hide them as a footman set another pot of tea down onto the table before her. Her husband, pale and quiet, covered her hand with his own.

"Please, *mo grá*," he murmured. "Listen to your family."

"I have made up my mind," she said firmly. "We've caused enough trouble."

At her feet, Turnip stood on his hind legs and pawed at her knees, wanting a bite of her roll.

"Don't," Gareth warned, rubbing at tired eyes. "His stomach's upset. Had me up all night."

"Another reason to take him back with us," Nerissa said brusquely.

And in the nursery upstairs the eldest of the de Montforte cousins, following a visit from their Aunt Eva, huddled together on the rug. Once Nurse went to tend to baby Aidan and Laura's little brother, Justin, Gabriel was quick to whisper instructions while the woman was briefly out of earshot.

"But I'm afraid," Mary said, her dark brown eyes huge with apprehension. "Everyone will be so angry..."

Gabriel shook his head. "If I were small enough I'd do it myself. I'm not afraid to get in trouble."

"I'm not afraid, either, but it doesn't seem right to make everyone worry so."

Charlotte, to whom the others naturally looked up given she was the eldest of them all, laid a reassuring hand on Mary's shoulder. "Do you want them to go home? After they only just got here?"

"Of course not, but..." She looked bleakly at the others. "Why does it have to be me?"

"Because Aunt Eva said it has to be you."

"Aunt Eva didn't exactly tell us to do this."

"No, but she ... well, she gave us the idea, didn't she?"

The children were silent, remembering the duchess sweeping into the nursery, her eyes full of mischief.

"I have come to tell you all that today will be a day of parting," she'd announced sorrowfully, to a clamor of "*nooo*s!" and protests and stricken faces. "It seems that Uncle Charles will be going back to Lynmouth Park along with you and your family, Mary, and Aunt Nerissa is returning to America."

"Why?"

"They just arrived!"

"We're only just getting to know Uncle Ruaidri! He's

funny!"

"He taught me how to make knots!"

"He took me fishing in the moat!

Tears welled in little Mary's eyes. "He rescued my kitten!"

"'Tis a pity, isn't it?" Aunt Eva had shaken her head and moved to the window to look out toward the stables. "Too bad that one of you, perhaps you, Mary ... couldn't just ... oh, I don't know ... hide in a trunk, or in the boot of the coach and ... disappear. Something that would force them to miss the stage and come back. It would certainly give your Uncle Lucien and me more time to figure out how to ... how to make everyone happy together."

"What she means is that Uncle Charles doesn't like Uncle Ruaidri," Gabriel had said baldly.

"Now, Gabriel," Charlotte scolded him.

"Well, it's not as if it isn't obvious, or the truth. We all saw them coming to fisticuffs, didn't we?"

"Enough of that," the duchess said. "I just wanted to prepare you all for a parting ... I leave it up to you to ... to decide how you might, well—" she had given them a secretive little wink—"*prevent* it."

Now, the children listened to Nurse in the next room tending to littlest ones of their group, including Aidan, who would soon be gone from them.

"They might never come back," Laura said.

Charlotte nodded. "Only we can stop them."

"It's up to us." Gabriel announced importantly. "And Mary, it has to be you. Aidan's too young, Laura probably is too. You're one of the three oldest of us and you're also the smallest."

"But ... I don't want to get in trouble."

Gabriel's eyes were sparkling with merriment. "If you do, I promise I will volunteer to take your punishment." He paused as Nurse hustled back in, and looked at them each in turn. "Now, are we doing this or not?"

Chapter Twenty

Charles stayed upstairs with Amy and his new son as long as he could without appearing rude.

He saw the coach being brought out of the stables, and Lucien's matched team, groomed to a sheen, shaking their heads and jangling their harnesses in their eagerness to be off. He heard the clamor of voices downstairs, felt the heavy energy of sorrow, heard the puppy barking.

"We should at least go say goodbye," Amy said, getting up from the bed. She had been nursing the baby, and the sorrow that seemed to permeate the very walls of the castle was reflected in her face, her eyes, her voice. "It's rude to stay up here. I'm going down."

Charles sat and put his head in his hands. He did not speak.

"Come with me, Charles. It will be your last chance," she said softly.

He hooked his arms around the back of his neck and stared down at the rug, saying nothing.

She moved close, bent down, and passed little Simon to him. He caught her eye as she did so, and the look on her face made his heart break all the more. He turned away, unable to bear the sorrow and regret he saw there, and with the baby in his arms, stared out the window at the clouds scudding across a blue, blue sky. What was there to say?

She made her way out of the room. She, who would not let her sister-in-law and family leave without a proper goodbye.

Charles took a deep breath, got to his feet, and with Simon cradled to his chest, went to the window. Down on the drive below, footmen carried trunks—most of which probably hadn't even been fully unpacked, he thought sadly—out of the house and to the waiting coach. Another footman was letting down the steps, and a groom held the waiting team.

Bugger it all.

He turned and left the room.

He was halfway down the stairs when he met Ruaidri O'Devir, moving painfully, just coming up.

"Good morning," Charles said stiffly, not knowing what else to say.

"Mornin', Lord Charles." The other man smiled. "I was just coming up to say goodbye. And thank ye for savin' me life last night."

Charles just looked away.

"Listen," the Irishman said, leaning against the wall behind him, "I know you and I didn't get off on the right foot ... I just wanted ye to know, I've no hard feelings."

"None here, either," Charles murmured, still looking away.

The Irishman put out a hand. "Until next time, brother."

Charles looked at the offered hand for a moment, then took it. "Until next time, Captain O'Devir."

The other man turned and made his way back down the stairs. Charles watched him go, his keen eyes noticing much. That Ruaidri O'Devir was in more pain than he was letting on. That he was limping when he reached the downstairs floor and trying very hard to hide it. Several hours in a coach—because why else had Lucien had the boot affixed to his vehicle unless he planned to have Nerissa and her family driven all the way back to the coast so they wouldn't have to take the stage?—was no good for a man who had nearly been killed just hours before, no good at all.

Charles started back down the stairs.

He caught up to them all as they were gathering in the Great Hall and heading out the great medieval doors, both of which were standing open to frame the coach and team outside on the drive. The household staff lined the steps, some of them in tears. Charlotte and Gabriel stood on either side of their father, Charlotte holding his hand, Gabriel looking down at the dirt and kicking aimlessly at a pebble. Baby Aidan was being passed around and given a final kiss on the cheek, a last hug, just one more cuddle. The puppy looked downcast for once and was quiet as he looked up at the adults above him. Captain O'Devir moved around the circle of family members, shaking hands and allowing a quick embrace by the women, and then it was Nerissa's turn. Nerissa, proud and composed, no longer the young, innocent girl he'd grown up with, Nerissa, a grown woman now with her own family, Nerissa who, according to servants' gossip, was the one who had made the decision to take her family back home.

Nerissa, not Ruaidri O'Devir.

She, the girl that he and his brothers had spent a lifetime protecting, was now protecting her beloved husband.

A de Montforte, through and through.

Leaving.

Charles glanced up at Lucien. His brother stood with the others, implacable as always, watching the farewells behind an inscrutable gaze. The duke remained that way as Eva embraced Nerissa and then moved to O'Devir, her hand on his shoulder as she murmured words of farewell.

Again, Charles glanced at Lucien, his heartbeat quickening as his desperation rose.

Do something, Charles thought.

Lucien, though, did nothing.

Nerissa turned and moved toward the coach, Aidan back in her arms. She looked up at Charles, and in her eyes, Charles saw the hurt, the sadness, and the sudden awful realization that he would probably never see her again. She did not come running back to say goodbye. She did not say a word to him. She merely turned and continued her steps toward the waiting vehicle. O'Devir handed her up and the coach settled on its well-oiled springs as the Irishman followed her inside, calling for the puppy.

Damn it, Lucien, do something!

The footmen climbed aboard, the coachman hoisted himself up, and the duke himself walked forward and shut the door.

"Goodbye, Lucien."

"Farewell and be safe."

"Goodbye!"

"Oh, goodbye!"

"I love you, Auntie Nerissa! Love you, Uncle Ruaidri!"

"Please come back soon!"

Each voice was a knife to Charles's heart. He willed his feet to move, but they would not. The driver picked up the reins and clicked to the horses and now the coach was moving away, wheeling around the drive, heading out past the row of old copper beeches, over the bridge of the moat and through the gatehouse. The puppy began barking from inside, its mischievous little face pressed against the glass. The team's hoofbeats began to fade as the conveyance drew farther away. Watching it, Amy and Juliet stood together, tears streaming down Amy's face, Juliet hugging her in quiet, shared sorrow. Andrew and Celsie turned and went back into the house, Gabriel and Charlotte trudging dejectedly in their wake. Gareth picked up little Laura, and with his niece's arms wrapped around his neck, slowly climbed the steps after them.

And Lucien, with Eva beside him as they watched the coach grow smaller and smaller, stood still and unmoving.

The puppy's yapping grew faint, then disappeared altogether until the only noise was the whisper of wind through the copper beeches.

A moment later, the coach was gone from sight, lost beyond the trees as it headed out onto the road that would take it to Ravenscombe, the coast, and finally, back to America.

&

BACK INSIDE, the mood was dark and empty and worse than awful. The energy that had lit the ancient home, even for a short time with Nerissa's and her family's arrival, was gone, sucked away like shells clawed back by an outgoing tide and leaving gloom and sorrow in its midst. Nobody said much.

They must all hate me, Charles thought. *And I don't blame them.*

He cleared his throat. "Amy, I think it's time to go as well. Are you all packed?"

Unlike with his sister's departure, there was no clamor, no sudden outcry. All sorrow must have been expended with Nerissa's parting. Or maybe they were all just glad to see him go.

"I'll just need a few moments," she said quietly, and turned and went upstairs.

Gareth and Andrew walked past him, neither of them looking at him. Lucien said something about his morning walk, previously delayed, which he now felt compelled to undertake. Gabriel ran off, his sad mood quickly abandoned, giggling now ... so much like his father, Charles thought, never serious, always in a good mood. Charlotte, taking the hands of Laura and Augustus, adjusting her stride for the younger children as she led them out of the Great Hall.

And from upstairs, a scream.

Amy's.

"*Charles!*"

He turned and ran for the stairs.

"Charles, come quickly!"

He took the steps three at a time, ran headlong down the corridor, and charged into his old apartments. There he found his wife, stricken and white-faced, frantically pulling back the covers on the bed, dropping to her hands and knees to peer under the furniture, rushing to the windows to haul aside the drapery and look behind them.

"Amy, what are you doing? You should be resting, not—"

"Mary! She's gone!"

"What?"

"She's missing! Nurse just came to ask where she went, because she thought she was with us, out on the drive, saying goodbye, but—"

"She wasn't with us," Charles said, feeling the blood drain from his face.

"Mary!" Amy screamed. "Mary!"

Charles spun on his heel and there was Lucien, leaning against the door. He raised an imperious brow. "Another crisis, Charles?"

"Mary is missing!"

"No, she's not."

"What do you mean?"

"I have just been ... informed that she is in my

coach. Which is exactly where I suspected she would be."

"What? Your coach?"

"Well, of course. You see, it appears the ... children had a plan to keep Nerissa and you both here, and spirited our dear Mary aboard the coach. I do believe you'll find her in the boot."

"*What!*"

"Yes, the boot."

Charles' mouth fell open. "The children were responsible for this? Their doing? You were the one who had the boot affixed to that vehicle. This was *your* plan, wasn't it?"

Lucien shrugged. "I daresay you should go rescue your daughter, Charles."

Behind him, Amy sat on the bed and put her head in her hands. Was she crying? Or laughing? Was she part of this ... this *scheme*, as well? Who else knew? Did Nerissa and Ruaidri? Was he to be made the laughingstock of the entire family?

"No, no, my dear Charles, your sister and husband do not know they have a little stowaway," Lucien drawled, reading his mind. "They will probably discover her, though, when they stop for the night."

"Damn you," Charles snarled. "Using our daughter for one of your dastardly machinations!"

Young Gabriel, looking so much like the little devil his father had been at the same age, was suddenly there beside Lucien. His arms were folded over his puffed-out chest, and he had a defiant gleam in his eye. "Uncle Charles," he said archly, and Charles could see his nephew was trying, unsuccessfully, not to laugh, "You mustn't blame Uncle Lucien or Aunt Eva for—"

"*Eva* was involved in this as well?"

The boy ignored him. "As I was saying, Uncle Charles, you mustn't blame them for Mary's actions. It was I who put her up to it."

"*You!*"

"Well, yes. I told her that I'd give her my favorite toy soldier, the one that looks like you, the one she's always wanted, if she were to sneak into the boot without anyone knowing."

Charles's mouth had dropped to the level of his abdomen. "*What!?*"

"Honestly, is that the only remaining word in your vocabulary?" Lucien murmured. "And here you have an Oxford education..."

"Damn it all—"

"Oh, Uncle Charles, please don't be cross with Mary. She only agreed to do it if I took her punishment. She is not to blame."

Juliet was suddenly there, as well as Celsie, Andrew, Gareth, and Eva. Behind them, Laura and Charlotte stood, and Charles saw the girl, trying to look neutral, unruffled, and concerned, was trying very hard to keep from grinning. She caught him staring at her, and looking down to mask her emotions, took Laura's and Gabriel's hands and led the children away.

Amy, on the bed, who may or may not have been implicit in this ... *scheme*. His brothers and their wives clustered around the door.

And Lucien, who straightened, pulled out his watch, and made a big show of consulting it.

He looked up at Charles, his face perfectly expressionless save for the faintest of smirks just touching one corner of his mouth.

"Better get going, Charles. I still have my walk to undertake, and it would be nice if you're all back for lunch."

❧

NERISSA, holding back tears, sat staring miserably out at the passing landscape. The noble, timeless downs dotted with sheep ... the white chalk mud of the verge ... rabbits sitting up on their haunches and watching as they passed. Inside, the familiar velvet luxury of the coach, the polished glass of the windows, and the well-sprung ride. It was likely the last time she'd ever be in this coach that she had known forever.

A coach that, like everything else she was leaving behind, was part of her childhood. Her history. Her past.

Her very essence.

In moments, they'd be in Ravenscombe, where she would tell the coachman to take the vehicle and team back to Blackheath despite Lucien's insistence that they ride in style back to the coast. Where she and Ruaidri would instead take the stage. Where—

"Hold up there! I say, hold up there!"

Ruaidri reached for his pistol. "Highwaymen? In broad daylight?"

The coach slowed, and outside, Nerissa heard the tattoo of galloping hoofbeats. She exchanged glances with Ruaidri, and a moment later, the coach came to a stop.

She started to get up but was held in her seat by her husband and a warning glance. Her arms tightened around Aidan, who started to fuss.

"I'm glad I caught up with you before you got any farther," said the same voice outside.

Charles?

Ruaidri just looked at her and opened the door. The two stepped out onto the road.

"Did we forget something?" Nerissa asked coolly.

Her brother didn't say a word. Instead, he swung down from Contender. The horse had no saddle, and Charles left the thoroughbred standing there like the well-trained military steed that he was. He strode briskly to the rear of the coach and nodded to the two bewigged and liveried footmen. They looked at him quizzically, and quietly stepped down from their perch.

Charles went straight to the boot, and while Nerissa and Ruaidri, puzzled, looked on, yanked it open.

"Papa!"

Oh my God...

Nerissa, horrified, could only stare as her brother reached down and plucked his daughter from the small compartment, folding her close to his chest and stroking her hair. He was shaking, and in confusion, Ruaidri and Nerissa exchanged glances.

Ruaidri cleared his throat. "Lord Charles, we had no idea," he began.

"I know you didn't."

Nerissa hurried over to her brother and the child, whom he now set down. "Mary, sweetheart, whatever were you thinking?"

The little girl's eyes were huge, and she looked at her father, at her aunt, and at the puppy, who had appeared at the door of the carriage, tail wagging in frenzy.

"We didn't want you to go." Her eyes filled with tears and her lower lip trembled. "We thought that if one of us hid in the coach, someone would come after us and everyone could still be together."

"Was this your idea?" Charles asked, blinking in shock that his daughter could be involved in something so cunning.

Mary's eyes grew even larger, and she went silent.

"Mary?"

"It ... it was the idea of all of us," she whispered. "I was chosen because I was the smallest."

"And who chose you?"

Mary looked down and began kicking at the dirt.

"Don't push her, Charles," Nerissa said gently, and leaned down so she was at her niece's level. "It's quite all right, Mary. I think we all know who is behind this."

"Please don't get him in trouble," she suddenly blurted, looking up. "He meant well ... we all did."

"I am most certain that your Uncle Lucien will not get into trouble."

"But it was Gab—" She paused, clapping a hand to her mouth.

"Gabriel?"

"*Ahem.*"

All eyes turned to the coachman, who was trying to maintain suitable decorum but whose face was starting to redden. "I am sworn to secrecy," he said hesitantly, "but I will say that young Gabriel was not the person who ... who had a word with me early this morning that we would have a stowaway on board."

Charles let out a long-suffering sigh, raked a hand through his hair, and leaned against the rear wheel of the coach. He looked at his daughter, who was clutching a toy soldier in her small fist. She reminded him of a fawn facing down a pack of wolves with nowhere to run. He looked at his sister, whose stunned face proclaimed her own ignorance of this whole scheme. And then he looked at his brother-in-law.

Ruaidri O'Devir gave him a wide grin and slowly began to laugh.

A few shy giggles escaped young Mary as she looked anxiously between the adults.

The coachman wiped at his own mouth, trying helplessly to suppress his own mirth, and then Nerissa burst out laughing as well.

"Devil take it," Charles muttered and then he, too, found himself laughing as he considered the lengths to which his own family had gone in order to make things right.

In order to keep them all together.

Together.

Hoofbeats sounded in the road behind them, and

they all turned to see Lucien, sitting astride his hellish black stallion.

"My dear me," he murmured, a little smile playing about his face. "Judging by the smiles and laughter, I'm assuming that amends have been made, all is well, and you're both ready to start over?"

Ruaidri looked at Charles and put out his hand. "Here's to second chances," he said amiably. "If ye're willin' to give me one."

Charles took the other man's hand and gripped it tightly. "I have been abominable," he said for all to hear. "My own pride and confusion kept me from seeing the truth. That you and my little sister love each other more than I could ever have imagined. That you would do anything for not only her, but her family back here in England, as you proved over and over for the short time that you have been here." He swallowed hard. "I am sorry, Captain O'Devir. I, too, would like to start over. To welcome you properly to the family."

"Ruaidri," the Irishman said. "Just Ruaidri, Lord Charles."

"Charles," the Englishman said. "Just Charles, Ruaidri."

The two exchanged grins and Nerissa, watching them, knew then that everything was going to be all right, after all.

Lucien sat atop his stallion, a triumphant little grin playing about his mouth. "Well then, that settles it, doesn't it?"

The puppy chose that moment to bounce down from the coach, and without a backwards glance, bolted back down the road from the direction they had all come.

Back toward Blackheath Castle.

Back, Nerissa thought, wiping at a tear, toward home.

Epilogue

With Lucien leading the way astride Armageddon, they arrived back at Blackheath to a small crowd. Servants, family, children, and dogs, even Mary's kitten, now safely cradled in Charlotte's arms—they were all there, and they sent up a rousing *hip hip, huzzah!* as Armageddon's shod hooves clattered over the moat's bridge, the coach right behind him.

Gabriel, running headlong, was the first to reach the vehicle as it came to a stop in front of the ancient, iron-banded doors.

"It worked!" he crowed. "Mary, you did it!"

She just smiled shyly and ran to her mother, who folded her in her arms and hugged her tight.

Charles swung down from Contender and handed the reins to a groom. He cleared his throat and waited for the clamor to subside, and his sister and her family to alight from the coach.

"Everyone," he said loudly. "If I might have your attention."

Voices stilled, and the small crowd looked at him, some in confusion, some in anticipation, one or two in worry. Lucien, still high atop his stallion, was gazing at something in the grass near the door.

"I want it to be known that from this day forward, I

welcome Ruaidri O'Devir into this family with the same warmth, affection, and commitment that the rest of you have done. I have been an absolute boor, unwilling to give my new brother the chance he deserved, unwilling, even, to accept that my little sister has the right to make her own choices and set the course for her own life. She is all grown up now, and it has been hard for me to see that. To acknowledge it. To accept that her protector is no longer a brother but a husband. Ruaidri has proven his love for her, and he has done more for this family in the few days that he's been here than some have done in a lifetime." He turned to Ruaidri, who looked a bit uncomfortable. "Ruaidri, I apologized earlier, but I wanted these words said for all to hear. Welcome to the family."

More cheers, and Ruaidri bowed his head in acknowledgement of his brother-in-law's earnest apology.

"You're not still leaving, are you, Uncle Charles?"

Charles flashed a smile. "No, Laura, we are not. And neither are Aunt Nerissa and Uncle Ruaidri and little Aidan. I think it's safe to say we're all starting over."

Reaching down to hug little Mary, he made his way to the house. Lucien's gaze went again to the spot in the grass toward which his brother was heading, his brother who had managed to salvage both his pride and his relationship with his sister and her husband, his rather stiff, rather upstanding brother who didn't see—

"*What the—*"

Lucien merely arched a brow and stifled a grin as Charles's shoe slid in the grass and he went down in a heap, landing hard on his bottom.

"That infernal puppy!"

The children howled with laughter as their uncle, the taciturn military officer who was always so serious and dignified, hurriedly got to his feet. He took a step, frowned, and then lifted his foot, grimacing as he examined the bottom of his shoe.

Gareth was snickering, Andrew's mouth was twitching, and even Lucien's dark eyes were sparkling with mischief.

"Guess we missed one," Gareth said, without contrition.

Charles started to head to the boot scraper mounted on the steps when Lucien's voice drifted down from aboard Armageddon.

"I daresay, Charles, there is something in that ... pile, that bears closer inspection," he murmured.

"What?"

"The dog shit," Ruaidri whispered, leaning close so the children couldn't hear. "There's something in it."

Charles opened his mouth, shocked. He looked up at Lucien. "You want me to go digging in ... in dog diarrhea?"

"Get your uncle a stick, Gabriel," Lucien said, and the boy ran to the copper beech that had broken the night before, its great limb still sprawled over the grass, the russet leaves already beginning to curl. He snapped off a branch, raced back to the group, and offered the stick to Charles.

"What is it, Uncle Charles?"

Laura, Mary, and even Charlotte, wrinkling her nose, moved forward, watching as their proud, dignified uncle took the stick and started poking around in puppy poop.

"I'll be d—" Charles caught himself before he could curse in the presence of women and children. "Is that—"

"Sure looks like it from up here," Lucien drawled.

Charles dug the stick into the grass and lifted something high, his mouth falling open.

"It's Mama's ring!" Mary cried.

"How did it get in ... in puppy poop?" Laura asked, stepping backward in horror.

"My dear children," Lucien said smoothly. "Little

Turnip ate everything else he could find. And he was still in the room where the ring was set on the table when most of us retired for the night. It's obvious his stomach is where the ring has been the entire time."

The children squealed, proper exclamations of disgust were made, and a servant, holding his nose, stepped forward and accepted the stick from Lord Charles on which hung the priceless band of gold and the jewels that encrusted it.

"I will take care of this and see that it is properly ... cleaned, my lord ... your Grace."

"Thank you, Puddyford."

Lucien swung down from the stallion, gave him over to a waiting groom, and headed toward the stairs, carefully avoiding the spot where Charles had come to such grief.

Two by two they went up the steps and then back into the ancient home that had witnessed births and deaths, weddings and funerals, the comings and goings and daily life of generations of de Montfortes. The children first, racing back into the castle with whooping, uncivilized cries of joy that had the adults pretending such behavior was to be lamented while they themselves held back such outward expressions of their own delight. Andrew and Celsie, with the puppy gnawing on the tongue of Andrew's shoe as he tried to move. Gareth and Juliet, glancing over their shoulders at Nerissa and Amy, who walked just behind them, and a few feet farther back, Charles and Ruaidri, sharing tentative grins as they followed the others inside.

"Let's have a second cup of tea, Ruaidri, and then it will be my pleasure to give you a proper tour of the house and grounds. I'll show you where Nerissa rode her first pony ... where the view of the downs is the very best ... where a long time ago, we found a hedgehog before we knew not to touch it and paid dearly for our curiosity."

"On horseback?" the Irishman asked, raising a brow.

"By God, no. We will walk. There is so much more to see on foot, don't you think?"

A distance behind them, the fifth duke and duchess of Blackheath, arms linked, followed, sharing a secret smile between them.

"Did you know that ring was in the dog's poop?" Eva asked. "Is that why you didn't have it cleaned up and allowed Charles to step in it?"

"My dear Eva ... there are many depths to which I might sink but that, I can assure you, is not one of them."

"I wonder," she said, giving him a sideways glance.

"In any case, the mystery is solved, our new brother is absolved, and that is that."

They paused, arm in arm, lingering a moment on the steps before heading inside to join the others. He drew her close, and she rested her head on his shoulder with a happy sigh.

"All's well that ends well," Eva said, with relief.

Lucien just smiled. "Ah, my dear... Nothing is ending," he murmured. "Indeed, I daresay it is just beginning."

— *The end* —

&a.

If you enjoyed this story, please consider posting a review on either Amazon, Goodreads, or whatever other forums you think are appropriate. Only a few lines are needed. Reviews are of enormous help to authors and are very much appreciated; thank you!

PREVIEW: THE WILD ONE

Prologue

Newman House, 18 April, 1775

My dear brother, Lucien,

It has just gone dark and as I pen these words to you, an air of rising tension hangs above this troubled town. Tonight, several regiments—including mine, the King's Own—have been ordered by General Gage, commander in chief of our forces here in Boston, out to Concord to seize and destroy a significant store of arms and munitions that the rebels have secreted there. Due to the clandestine nature of this assignment, I have ordered my batman, Billingshurst, to withhold the posting of this letter until the morrow, when the mission will have been completed and secrecy will no longer be of concern.

Although it is my most ardent hope that no blood will be shed on either side during this endeavour, I find that my heart, in these final moments before I must leave, is restless and uneasy. It is not for myself that I am afraid, but another. As you know from my previous letters home, I have met a young woman here with whom I have become attached in a warm friendship. I suspect you do not approve of my becoming so enamoured of a storekeeper's daughter, but things are different in this place, and when a fellow is three thousand miles away from home, love makes a far more desirable companion than loneliness. My dear Miss Paige has made me happy, Lucien, and earlier tonight, she accepted my plea for her hand in marriage; I beg you to understand, and forgive, for I know that someday when you meet her, you will love her as I do.

My brother, I have but one thing to ask of you, and knowing that you will see to my wishes is the only thing that calms my troubled soul during these last few mo-

ments before we depart. If anything should happen to me—tonight, tomorrow, or at any time whilst I am here in Boston—I beg of you to find it in your heart to show charity and kindness to my angel, my Juliet, for she means the world to me. I know you will take care of her if ever I cannot. Do this for me and I shall be happy, Lucien.

I must close now, as the others are gathered downstairs in the parlour, and we are all ready to move. May God bless and keep you, my dear brother, and Gareth, Andrew, and sweet Nerissa, too.

Charles

Sometime during the last hour, it had begun to grow dark.

Lucien de Montforte turned the letter over in his hands, his gaze shuttered, his mind far away as he stared out the window over the downs that stood like sentinels against the fading twilight. A breath of pink still glowed in the western sky, but it would soon be gone. He hated this time of night, this still and lonely hour just after sunset when old ghosts were near, and distant memories welled up in the heart with the poignant nearness of yesterday, close enough to see yet always too elusive to touch.

But the letter was real. Too real.

He ran a thumb over the heavy vellum, the bold, elegant script that had been so distinctive of Charles's style—both on paper, in thought, and on the field—still looking as fresh as if it had been written yesterday, not last April. His own name was there on the front: *To His Grace the Duke of Blackheath, Blackheath Castle, nr. Ravenscombe, Berkshire, England.*

They were probably the last words Charles had ever written.

Carefully, he folded the letter along creases that had become fragile and well-worn. The blob of red wax with which his brother had sealed the letter came together at the edges like a wound that had never healed, and try as he might to avoid seeing them, his gaze caught the words that someone, probably Billingshurst, had written on the back.

Found on the desk of Captain Lord Charles Adair de Montforte on the 19th of April 1775, the day on which his lordship was killed in the fighting at Concord. Please deliver to addressee.

A pang went through him. Dead, gone, and all but forgotten, just like that.

The Duke of Blackheath carefully laid the letter inside the drawer, which he shut and locked. He gazed once more out the window, lord of all he surveyed but unable to master his own bitter emptiness. A mile away, at the foot of the downs, he could just see the lights of Ravenscombe village, could envision its ancient church with its Norman tower and tombs of de Montforte dead. And there, inside, high on the stone wall of the chancel, was the simple bronze plaque that was all they had to tell posterity that his brother had ever even lived.

Charles, the second son.

God help them all if anything happened to him, Lucien, and the dukedom passed to the third.

No. God would not be so cruel.

He snuffed the single candle and with the darkness enclosing him, the sky still glowing beyond the window, moved from the room.

Also by Danelle Harmon

Introducing
The Bestselling, Award-Winning, Critically Acclaimed
DE MONTFORTE BROTHERS SERIES

"The bluest of blood; the boldest of hearts;
the de Montforte brothers will take your breath away."

 # 1 Kindle Store bestseller: The Wild One

The Wild One

The Beloved One

The Defiant One

The Wicked One

The Wayward One

The Admiral's Heart

The Fox & the Angel

My First Noel

The Homecoming

HEROES OF THE SEA SERIES

Master of My Dreams

Captain of My Heart

My Lady Pirate

Taken by Storm

Wicked at Heart

Lord of the Sea

Heir to the Sea

Never Too Late for Love

Scandal at Christmas

My Saving Grace

Pirate in My Arms

About the Author

New York Times and *USA Today* bestselling author Danelle Harmon has written twenty-one critically acclaimed and award-winning books, with many being published all over the world and translated into numerous languages. She and her family make their home in New England with numerous animals including four dogs, an Egyptian Arabian horse, and a flock of pet chickens. Danelle enjoys reading, spending time with family, friends and her pets, and sailing her Melonseed skiff, *Kestrel II*. She welcomes email from her readers and can be reached at Danelle@danelleharmon.com or through any of the means listed below:

CONNECT WITH ME ONLINE!

Danelle Harmon's Website

Want to know when the next new title from Danelle is released? Click here!

Even more ways to connect:

www.ingramcontent.com/pod-product-compliance
Lightning Source LLC
Chambersburg PA
CBHW020148120726
47903CB00007B/2454